A Dirty Deed

A Dirty Deed

by Ted Stenhouse

Kids Can Press

Kids Can Press acknowledges the financial support of the Ontario Arts Council,
the Canada Council for the Arts and the Government of Canada, through the
BPIDP, for our publishing activity.

Published in Canada by
Kids Can Press Ltd.
29 Birch Avenue
Toronto, ON M4V 1E2

Published in the U.S. by
Kids Can Press Ltd.
2250 Military Road
Tonawanda, NY 14150

www.kidscanpress.com

Edited by Charis Wahl
Designed by Julia Naimska

Printed and bound in Canada

CM 03 0 9 8 7 6 5 4 3 2 1
CM PA 03 0 9 8 7 6 5 4 3 2 1

National Library of Canada Cataloguing in Publication Data

Stenhouse, Ted
    A dirty deed / Ted Stenhouse

ISBN 1-55337-360-X (bound).   ISBN 1-55337-361-8 (pbk.)

    I. Title.

PS8587.T4485D42 2003   jC813'.6   C2002-902605-9
PZ7

Kids Can Press is a *Corus*™ Entertainment company

To Mom
for the journey we shared,
the goodness you left with the memories of those you passed,
and the quiet kindness your heart placed in mine

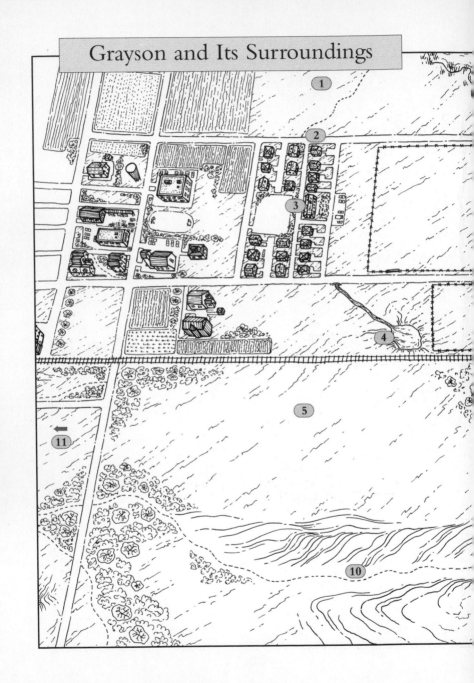

Grayson and Its Surroundings

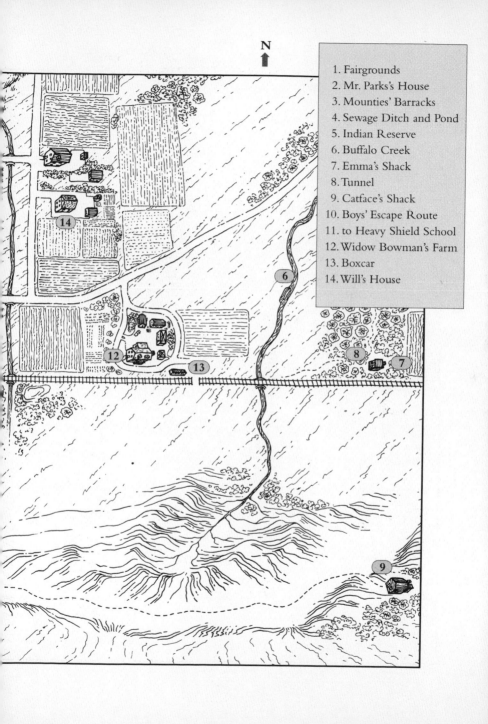

N

1. Fairgrounds
2. Mr. Parks's House
3. Mounties' Barracks
4. Sewage Ditch and Pond
5. Indian Reserve
6. Buffalo Creek
7. Emma's Shack
8. Tunnel
9. Catface's Shack
10. Boys' Escape Route
11. to Heavy Shield School
12. Widow Bowman's Farm
13. Boxcar
14. Will's House

Stars Don't Fall

I could feel the heat from Arthur's shoulder next to mine and the damp sweat that was different from my own, and even though we'd been friends forever, I could still smell he was an Indian. I never thought much about this being a bad thing. Sometimes smells even bring back memories. The problem is memories could be either good or bad. And being reminded that we were different usually brought back the bad memories, like the town people going out of their way to make an Indian's life miserable, for no other reason than because he talked different or looked different or smelled different or a hundred other reasons that made even less sense.

I took a few easy breaths, trying to forget how ashamed I was to be white, and went back to watching the night sky.

"Hey, Will Samson," Arthur said, pushing my arm, "are you dreaming again?"

"Just thinking."

"Thinking causes nothing but trouble. Remember what Mr. Parks did when he caught you thinking in his class."

"Yeah," I said. "He passed me to grade seven when I figured I'd be in grade six for the rest of my life."

"I'm glad I don't have to think to pass."

Arthur wasn't *really* glad. He was just making a smart remark about Heavy Shield School, where they make Indians into white men. He always said that the easiest way to turn an Indian into a white man was by taking away the Indian's common sense, so he couldn't think for himself.

I moved my shoulders against the prairie grass.

"I've been looking up for an hour and I haven't seen any stars fall," Arthur said, and pointed. "But that one over there looks like it could be loosening up a bit."

"Stars don't fall, Arthur. Or loosen up."

"What do they do?" I could feel Arthur grinning. "I know. They shoot."

"Stars don't do anything. They just stay put forever and burn."

"What are we doing out here then? My eyes are starting to hurt from staring at all this darkness."

"We're waiting for a meteor shower. Just like Mr. Parks told us — this morning, at the post office. Boy, you sure have a bad memory."

"The teachers at Heavy Shield School took it away from me. They said it was their duty — the Treaty said so."

"I don't want to talk about treaties. I'm tired of them. Besides, they don't have anything to do with Mr. Parks. He's the best teacher Grayson ever had."

Arthur stretched out his arms, then locked his fingers together and slipped them under his head.

I moved over to make room for his elbows.

I wished Arthur went to my school. I could see nothing but fun in it, being that we were in the same grade and all. But that wasn't going to happen in our lifetime. I didn't believe Arthur when he said the white people at Heavy Shield School were taking away the Indians' common sense. But whatever they were doing to the Indian kids, I did wonder why it had to be done where nobody could see.

I locked my fingers together and put them behind my head just like Arthur had done. Then I thought about Mr. Parks.

"So who's the best teacher in your school?" I asked.

"The one who quits and goes back to the city."

"What about that old guy with the prune face?"

"He tied with the one who goes back to the city."

"So you do have a best teacher."

"No," Arthur said. "Old Prune Face died."

I was just about to say I never heard of any Indian kid liking any teachers, so one of them quitting or dying would cause a good deal of back-slapping and yahooing. But Arthur sat up and pointed to the eastern sky.

"There goes one now."

"That's not a meteor. It's a flying saucer."

"A flying saucer?"

"Sure," I said. "Fresh from Mars. With a load of new teachers for Heavy Shield School."

Arthur lay back down and let out a big sigh. "I don't know why I hang around with you."

"Yes you do. We like doing the same things."

"Like fishin'," Arthur said before I could.

"And duck huntin' in the fall."

"Then there's goose huntin' when somebody else digs the pit."

"And goin' into the post office at noon, when it's full of town ladies, and letting out a real stinker."

"Then giving the ladies a suspicious look, like they did it."

I started laughing, and a second later Arthur was laughing and talking at the same time.

"Remember three Saturdays ago when you tried to sneak out one you'd been saving for nearly half a day?" He had to catch his breath before he went on. "And when you finally let it go, it sounded like a thunderstorm had hit inside the post office. And the calendar flipped all its pictures clear back to the start of the year, and in the January picture was a farmer standing by an old barn with snow everywhere and the big doors open, like he was gettin' rid of a horrible smell."

"You tell bigger whoppers than my dad."

Arthur rolled sideways and grabbed his stomach. He was laughing so hard he'd stopped making any sound at all. Pretty soon, the muscles in my face were all knotted up, and I thought I'd die if I didn't get some air soon.

Every time I figured we were done, Arthur would snicker and we'd start all over again.

We were just about laughed out when Arthur sat up with a jerk. "Quiet," he said. "There's something coming this way."

"Another flying saucer?"

He just stared out into the night.

In a second, we were both sitting, watching three spots of yellow light jerking in the dark, flashing through the poplars and cattails and tall grass growing along the irrigation ditch — listening to the gagging bark of a dog tied with a rope, and the sound of running men.

What a Miserable Sound

"Look over there!" called a distant voice.

"I already looked, boss," a second one called back.

"Well look again."

The dog let out a bunch of barks and growls that ended when the man cussed. "We're not after a darned jackrabbit."

The dog yelped, then gagged.

"Whud'e'ya figure they're huntin'?" I asked.

"Not jackrabbits," Arthur answered.

I went to give him an elbow in the ribs but held up when he put his finger to his lips and jerked his head toward the sound.

"Where're you going?" I asked.

"Gotta get a closer look."

"I don't know," I said, grinning at Arthur's dark shape. "What if they mistake us for jackrabbits?"

"Then they'll be stupid, not just noisy."

He didn't wait for me to say anything smart or even go for his ribs again. He just tipped forward, half onto his hands and knees, and crawled down the short hill, through the dry prairie grass, up the other side to the slope of rocks that held the train tracks. I followed.

I leaned my elbows on the cool steel and looked over the rails like Arthur did. "Could be a deer, I suppose."

"Maybe they wounded one and tracked it down here," Arthur said.

"I didn't hear any shots." When Arthur didn't answer, I added, "I guess it's better to get shot being mistook for a deer than a jackrabbit."

Arthur went to give me an elbow in the ribs, but I got my arm in the way. His elbow hit mine and we both let out an "Ouch."

While Arthur rubbed the feeling back into his arm, a piece of cactus flopped back and forth on his shirt. It must've got caught there when he crawled down the hill.

I pulled it out and handed it to him.

Arthur nodded, took the cactus by one spine, and flipped it across the tracks. He gave his other sleeve a careful stroke, then stuck his head back above the rail and watched the men again.

They were about a quarter mile ahead and a hundred yards to the left. The yellow coal-oil lights flickered as the men searched behind a clump of poplars, crossed a clearing, stopped, and checked a patch of cattails. They made the same zigzag pattern on both banks, working their way toward us and the spot where the ditch got too wide and deep to cross —

where the trees and cattails ended and the grass got short and sunburned. They were slopping around in the water and cussing. Whatever they were hunting, they didn't care if it heard.

"Something oughtta flush soon." I was pretty excited. "I'll bet it'll come right out the end of all that tall grass." I pointed. "We better get ready to duck just in case they get crazy with shooting."

"The only way you'd get shot is if those men are hunting something that couldn't keep his mouth quiet to save his soul."

I gave Arthur a look.

He turned away, grinning as he gazed over the rail.

I lay almost touching Arthur's shoulder, the yellow coal-oil light flashing across his dark eyes as the lanterns swung in the men's hands. I expect the men were cussing because they were excited about night hunting. I like to cuss when I get excited.

As the men got close to the open ground, the dog let out a long, low howl.

Arthur gave me an easy nudge in the ribs and a shush for good measure as something burst from the side of the ditch and hit, running full-out, down the edge of the wheat field. It was a good size, but still too far away to say what it was.

"He's in the field!" somebody hollered.

The three lights bumped up and down and water slopped. Then the lights came together, almost making one.

"Get the son of a —" another voice hollered.

I knew that voice now. It belonged to Old Man Howe. Something pretty important was happening for Howe to be running around in the night.

"They're huntin' a person," Arthur said.

I went to give him an elbow for talking out loud, but held up. It *was* a person. But I judged it was a kid, not a man. I couldn't tell by looking, just by the sound he was making — a crying, begging sound. I didn't think bawling would do him much good. Howe would still give the kid a good whipping if he caught him.

"I'm pulling for the kid," I said.

"Me too."

"I don't like Old Man Howe."

"Me neither."

The shadow flashed through the field, getting closer to me and Arthur.

"Loewan!" Howe hollered. "You double back and cut him off if he tries to go for the ditch. And you," he said to the third man, "hit for the tracks and cut him off there. I'll go straight."

The dog barked like crazy.

"Shut up!" Howe hollered.

The dog shut up.

The lights took off in three directions.

Out in the wheat field, the kid had disappeared below the tall July grain. I couldn't see much more than shadows, but I'd bet he'd dropped to his hands and knees and was crawling as fast as he could. He might've been out of sight, but he was crying and begging worse than ever. What a miserable sound.

"Old Man Howe," Arthur said.

"And Albert Loewan."

"Who's the other guy?"

"I don't know."

"Maybe one of Howe's hired hands?"

"I guess. He's got enough of them."

Albert Loewan was Howe's foreman. And Howe was the richest and meanest man in Grayson.

"If we get in line with them," Arthur said, "we'd be able to see better, and we could still keep the railway tracks between us for cover."

"Okay."

We slid down on our side of the rocks to where the grass started, ducked below the level of the rails, and hit for the irrigation ditch. After fifty yards, we reached the ditch bank. The water flowed from the Indian reserve behind us, gathered in a deep hole, then churned and boiled as it dropped into a big wooden culvert and crossed under the tracks.

Arthur crawled up the slope ahead of me and looked over the rail.

"They're going to get him," Arthur said.

I caught up just in time to see the kid jump straight out of the grain. He looked like a young deer that had hid for as long as his nerves could stand. But he jumped at the worst time — right in front of the third man.

"I got him!" the man hollered.

What's Another Beating to an Indian?

The man yanked the kid by the shirt and swung him around. The kid fell and rolled into the grain. As the man spun around, the coal-oil lantern made a yellow circle. The two remaining lights stopped, turned and came toward us through the field.

Howe was pretty fast even though he was close to eighty years old. The dog was strong and added a good deal to Howe's speed. Loewan was slow and fat, from drinking beer and sitting around telling other men how a job should be done.

"Hold him good!" Howe shouted. "Don't let him loose again!"

Albert Loewan was gasping for air.

The dog was half barking and half gagging as it pulled against the rope.

The kid was putting up a pretty good fight. If I was the third man, I would've put down the lantern and got a hold of the kid with both hands. I'd just thought that when the kid screamed and ripped out of his shirt. Now the third man was holding a shirt in one hand and a lantern in the other.

The kid stood for a long second, looking like he was going to grab his shirt back, but I expect he was frozen with fear.

They were about fifty yards away, and the lantern gave off enough light to see. There was no mistaking.

"The kid's an Indian," Arthur said.

"And he's going to get caught again if he doesn't get a move-on."

The kid's long body sliced through the wheat, with the man running after him. The lantern glowed bright as the oil slopped around the wick, and the shirt flapped in the wind of the man's own running.

Behind them, Howe was cussing the dog.

The kid broke from the field, crossed the short prairie grass, and turned to where me and Arthur had first seen the yellow lights. The man was closing fast. The kid glanced over his shoulder just as the man grabbed a handful of his hair and jerked him backward. But the kid broke the grip, made long stumbling steps, almost caught his balance, then landed face first in the rocks. The man stood over him, holding the lantern high in one hand as he whipped at him with the shirt. The kid scrambled up the rocks to the rails, then jumped to his feet. For half a second, he just glared down at the man.

"Let's see you outrun this!" the man hollered, giving the lantern a looping roundhouse throw.

The lantern flew over the kid toward Arthur and me, tumbling through the air making a spinning yellow arch, then hit the steel rail and burst into a big ball of flames.

I jumped back and plowed right into Arthur. Arthur didn't move, his eyes narrow as he stared straight ahead.

Through the growing flames, I could see the kid jerk his head back and forth between the man and the fire. The man laughed. But the kid ran right into the flames. The man cussed, rolled the shirt into a tight ball, and threw it at the kid.

When it got above the flames, it started to unroll, but the heat caught it and the shirt floated. For a second, it hung there and waved with its boneless sleeves. Then, *poof.* The shirt burst into flames and fell, twisting and turning down the rise of rails and ties and rocks, as bright as daylight.

"That's Catface," Arthur said. "And Kratz. The strap supervisor from Heavy Shield School."

"Who?"

The kid shot through the flames and caught a patch of fire-melted tar. His feet flew out in front of him, and he was down. Kratz was trying to make up his mind which side of the flames to circle when Howe and Loewan came charging out of the field.

"He's over there!" Kratz yelled, pointing to where Catface had gone down.

The dog came right up onto its back legs as it pulled against the rope.

"Get him while he's down," Howe said.

The kid got to his hands and knees, scrambled along the rocks, and stopped right in front of Arthur and me. He would've seen us if he hadn't been looking over his shoulder at the dog. His skin was shiny with sweat, and he smelled of pee. He started digging a hole along the edge of a tie. Then he pulled some folded papers from under his belt, stuffed them into the hole and pushed some rocks over them. A second later, he was looking right at us. His eyes were big and red, and a piece of cactus was stuck with its spines deep in his cheek. Blood trailed down his face.

In another second, he was running back toward the flames. It looked like he was leading the men away from the papers, but I was hoping he was giving Arthur and me a chance to get away. Howe and Loewan and Kratz were coming around the flames from the other direction. The kid ran right past them. All three men stood for a moment just watching the kid run.

Howe kicked Kratz. "You want to keep that job of yours, you'll get him."

Kratz took off down the tracks.

Loewan bent over, grabbed hold of his knees, and started coughing and choking. It sounded like he was going to die. Then he spit out something long and green. That seemed to help his breathing.

"You useless son of a —" Howe said. "You spit on my foot!"

The dog barked right in Loewan's face.

"Okay," Howe said, and slipped the rope over the dog's head. "Get goin'."

The dog sat there looking surprised.

Howe smacked his ear. "You're as stupid as Loewan here." He hit the dog again. "Get him!"

The dog took off down the tracks.

"Let's go," I said to Arthur. "I don't want to be here when Howe comes back for whatever is buried under those rocks."

"Just get a handful of rocks and cover me," Arthur said.

"What?"

"If Howe comes this way, start throwing rocks."

"What about the dog?"

"You better make sure you hit him a good one, right on the head."

Arthur rolled onto the tracks, dug out the papers, and stuffed them under his shirt.

I didn't need the rocks. The dog had the kid down, and Kratz had caught up to them and joined in, hollering at the dog and kicking at the kid. Howe and Loewan had just got there when Kratz landed a solid shot.

The dog yelped and fell over.

"You fool!" Howe shouted.

Arthur rolled back. "Let's get outta here."

"What about the kid?"

"His name is Catface."

"Okay. What about Catface?"

That's when I heard a scream — somewhere on the other side of the yellow flames.

"We can help him best by getting these papers to a safe place," Arthur said.

"Why take the papers? You figure Howe's doing all this for some stupid old papers?"

"No," Arthur said. "I figured he was after Catface's shirt all along."

"His shirt?"

Arthur tapped me on the forehead like he was knocking on a door. "It's not that hard to figure out."

I frowned and pushed his hand down. "I'm not stupid."

"Besides," he said after a few seconds. "Catface is an Indian. If Howe *is* after these papers, he'll beat Catface 'til he tells where he hid the papers."

I knew Arthur would stand with Catface just because they were both Indians. There was a good deal of nature in helping your own. But I didn't much like the idea of getting into a fight with Old Man Howe. He was as mean as he was rich.

"But when Catface tells Howe, and then Howe finds the papers gone, he'll figure Catface was lying," I said. "Then Catface will get a worse beating."

Arthur pulled out the papers and pushed them close to my face. "I've got to hold these for Catface."

"Howe will beat him worse than ever."

There was another awful scream.

"What's another beating to an Indian?" Arthur said, and gave me a mean look.

"Okay. Let's go."

Arthur was right. Old Man Howe would beat Catface good even if he found the papers. Then Catface would be beaten up *and* short some papers.

Arthur slid down the rocks to the grass, and crawled to the culvert. He held the papers high in one hand, stepped into the fast water, and disappeared under the railway tracks.

I slipped into the water behind him. It was kind of warm considering how cold I felt inside. The current carried us under the tracks north toward my house, and for about five minutes we drifted. We were a couple hundred yards downstream and just past the start of the trees when our feet caught a mud bar. There we turned to the shore and crawled out of the ditch, staying close to the bank, hiding among the cattails and poplars.

When I glanced over my shoulder, Howe and his men had Catface stripped naked, and they were looking through his pants and all over the ground. Catface kept trying to cover himself as they pushed him and pulled him and shook him. The anger and shame moved inside me like an animal. A second later the fear came.

"Come on," Arthur said as he jerked my arm.

"What if he tells Howe he saw us?"

"He won't tell on another Indian."

"What about me?"

"You better hope Catface doesn't know your name."

"I didn't know his name. So how could he know mine?"

I guess I sounded kind of scared, because Arthur said, "Howe wouldn't do that to a white kid." He tilted his head toward the screams. "He'd get in trouble."

"Okay. Let's get outta here before they come looking."

We crossed over the ditch bank and ran down the trail that headed straight up the lane to my house.

Behind us, Catface was screaming worse than ever.

Not Even the Crickets Talked

Arthur and I were behind my house in our special looking-at-the-stars spot in the tall grass, behind the outhouse and the lilac bush. Our clothes were hanging on the barbed-wire fence and we were trying to forget about Catface, at least until our clothes dried.

Around us was the circle we'd cut from the tall grass. Under our feet, the grass was spread out into a soft mat. On the east edge, almost under the fence, was an old potato sack stuffed with leftover grass tied with a piece of twine. It was nearly the perfect spot for two star-lookers to stretch out and rest their heads as they dreamed about comets and asteroids and whole other worlds.

"Figure there's somebody living up there?" I asked.

"Sure."

"Figure they look up and dream about us?"

"Why not?"

"Once I dreamed I lived up there, like it was my real home," I said. "And in that dream, I was dreaming what I figured was maybe the craziest dream a fellow could have in a place that was about as different from Grayson as a place could be."

"Did you dream yourself right back to Grayson, Alberta, in July 1952? Was it a dream about here and now?"

"Yes. But it had monsters in it."

I tried to think of the worst dream I'd ever had, then imagined what it would be like to live on a world like that. I wasn't having much luck, though. All I could think about was Catface standing naked, with the coal-oil fire burning as bright as daylight, and him trying to cover himself as Howe and his men jerked and pushed him.

My face felt hot, like it was me and not Catface who was being shamed.

We were just getting up when Old Man Howe pulled onto our lane. We dropped flat on the soft grass. I rolled back to the fence and reached for our clothes as the headlights from Howe's truck swung across my hand.

"They'll see them move," Arthur whispered, and jerked my arm down.

I dropped to the ground and lay dead still. I tried to slow my breathing, but it had already decided I should be running.

"Figure Howe saw us running up the lane?" I asked.

"He saw something."

Around us, the air smelled of engine exhaust.

Then came the knock on our back door and the sound of Howe's voice. "Evening, ma'am."

"Mr. Howe?" Mom said. "It's awful late. Is somebody hurt?" Her voice sounded like she was talking through bobby pins. She always took them out just before going to bed. I expect she wasn't too happy about having to put them all back in.

"Sorry to bother you at such an hour," he said. "But I'm kind of stuck for help to haul my wheat quota tomorrow. Can I talk to your boys?"

"He's lying to your mom," Arthur whispered.

"And a pretty good one, too," I said.

Before Mom could answer, there came a kid's muffled cry — like somebody was holding a hand over his mouth.

"Is that crying?" Mom asked.

"It's nothing, ma'am."

"What do you mean, nothing? How can a crying child be nothing?" I could hear her footsteps on our old wooden stairs as she pushed past Howe.

"Don't you go minding my business," Howe said.

"I can't let a hurt child go unattended."

"I'm here about work." Howe's voice got forceful. "Do those boys of yours want the work or not?"

"Good Lord!" Mom gasped. "He's naked."

"I caught him stealing, right in my own home."

"Well, if that's true, take him to Sergeant Findley."

"That's where we were going when I thought about your boys hauling grain for me tomorrow."

"You can do a lot of pretty important stuff all at once."

"Never mind the Indian. What about the work? Can I talk to your boys?"

"My boys are in bed. You should'a come by earlier."

"She's lying back," I whispered.

"And a pretty good one, too," Arthur said.

"Now what are you doing?" Howe asked. "Just leave him there. Don't go giving him your sweater. I'm hauling him to the Mounties right now."

"He's going covered."

Howe grumbled. His truck door slammed hard. The engine roared, and in a second the light was slicing through the tall grass, turning bright on the outhouse door, then sweeping across the house and out over the potato field. Howe turned right, up the road toward his farm.

We watched as his taillights disappeared.

"He's not going to the Mounties," Arthur whispered. "He's going someplace where he can give Catface an even worse beating."

"Did he figure I was really in the house, or was he just guessing?"

"I'd say he was guessing."

"So Catface didn't tell." Saying it made me feel better. "Besides, he doesn't know my name."

"If Catface told, Howe'd be in your house right now. Your mom couldn't stop him."

"She'd stop him."

I was just about to get up when the outhouse door squeaked open, then closed. It was Mom. She had stood in the dark and watched Howe drive up the road. Maybe she'd heard me and Arthur whispering. I'd bet she had, because it was a pretty quiet night.

I gave Arthur the shush sign and pointed to our half-dry clothes. He nodded back. We quietly pulled our clothes down and, still lying in the grass, got dressed.

We were half under the barbed wire into Mrs. Bowman's barley field when the outhouse door squeaked again. We froze and listened for Mom's footsteps. There weren't any. She must have been standing near the outhouse, listening for any sounds from Arthur and me, thinking about the crying kid.

Then she spoke. "Will, did you see Mr. Howe hurt that boy?"

Arthur elbowed me in the ribs.

I stayed quiet. All I could hear was my own breathing.

Then she asked, "Arthur, did you see Howe hurt that boy?"

I poked Arthur.

He stayed quiet.

Mom sighed. "Boys, Mr. Howe's rich. That means he's above the law or thinks he is. It's best to give a man like that what he wants." There was a long stretch of time where not even the crickets talked.

Finally she said, "And it's easier for him to get away with hurting Indians. This town does some shameful things, Arthur. I'm sorry for that."

I could hear her footsteps heading back to the house as me and Arthur slipped under the fence. After a hundred yards, we crossed back under the fence, circled our potato field on the north side of the house, turned left down the road and walked along the irrigation ditch, to the railway tracks, and on toward Arthur's house — where I had told Mom I was going for the night.

Along the way, Arthur asked, "Do you suppose she knew we were there, or was she just guessing?"

"I'd say she was guessing."

"I think she knew."

"Yeah, me too."

We walked until we got to the train station. There, we stood under the light above the sign that said "Grayson" and took out the papers. I was so excited my hands were shaking.

Before I could read a word, Arthur grabbed my arm and jerked it. "Trouble," he said.

Sergeant Findley drove down Main Street, stopped at the war memorial, then turned toward the train station and rolled slowly up the side street.

We crossed over to the reserve side of the tracks, crouched down, and headed for the path that ran through the low part that the Indians called Happy Valley. By the time Sergeant Findley was out of sight and we could look at the papers, we were a half a mile from the nearest light. I could hardly tell the paper was white. Arthur gave them a good shake to see if any money would fall out. None did. That made him suspicious.

Arthur figured that the only thing that would make these papers important to Mr. Howe was if there was money in them someplace. Knowing Mr. Howe like I did, I had to agree — the only thing he liked more than being mean was money.

It Was Hard Not to Make a Wish

The best time to look at stars is when the moon is with the sun and they're as far away from this side of the world as they can get. Like tonight.

At about one o'clock, we got to Arthur's house and settled into our third star-watching spot. It was awfully black out, and the stars were as beautiful as I could remember. That was too bad, because all I could think about was the paper hidden under Arthur's belt.

We sat on the blanket Arthur's mom had put out and spread the papers between us. Arthur turned them so they were in the starlight. He shook his head and put them back on the blanket. I rolled over onto my stomach and got my face so close to the pages that my eyelashes touched the paper.

"What does it say?" Arthur asked.

"I can't see. It's too dark."

"Maybe Howe has some money pasted on the paper."

I ran my fingers over the pages.

"Maybe on the back," Arthur said.

"I gave the pages a good scratching already. I couldn't feel any ridges."

"I wish we had electricity."

"Yeah," I said.

"You don't have electricity either."

"I know, but we got coal oil. I wish *you* had coal oil."

"We should'a told your mom we were hiding in the grass. Then we could'a gone into the house and checked what makes this paper so important."

"Mom would'a made us take it back to Mr. Howe."

"Why?" Arthur asked. "I heard her lie to him."

"Yeah, but she hates stealin' even worse than she hates Mr. Howe."

Arthur quickly pointed to the northeastern sky over Grayson. "There goes a good one. Maybe it'll hit Howe's farm."

"Nah. Mr. Parks said most meteors burn up in the atmosphere."

But it was a pretty good shooting star. Okay, a meteor. Mr. Parks had said there was going to be a big meteor shower starting at about two o'clock in the northeastern sky. He'd said it was caused by a comet that passed by maybe a million years ago. Maybe it even hit Earth and killed all the dinosaurs. Mr. Parks gets pretty excited about science. It rubbed off on me, and on Arthur a bit, too. Anyway, every time Earth gets in the same place where the comet was, before it killed the dinosaurs, we see a meteor shower. I guess this would be about the millionth time.

"There goes another one," Arthur said. "Did you make a wish?"

"You don't make a wish on science. Wishing is superstition."

"I wished I knew why an Indian would want a piece of paper — or anything at all from Old Man Howe."

I didn't tell Arthur, but I *had* made a wish. I wished I knew why Howe was so worried about a piece of paper that was just words and not even money.

I folded the papers and stuffed them under one corner of the blanket. A smell of wood smoke came off the blanket when I patted it flat. It smelled like breakfast.

Then I said, "Maybe we can figure out something about Catface without knowing anything about the paper. And then maybe figure out something about the paper and even Mr. Howe."

A pair of meteors streaked overhead.

"Did you wish?" I asked.

"Yeah, I wished you'd quit trying to figure out people by using science."

"Okay, so why don't you sneak into the house and get some matches, and we'll go back and set fire to those fence posts we stacked for my dad yesterday. We wouldn't have any problem reading the paper then."

"Mom will catch me. She hears everything. She's probably listening to us now."

"So what?"

"She hates stealing even worse than your mom does. Howe will have these papers back before morning. And anyway —" Arthur grinned and shook his head.

"What?"

"If we burned down your dad's fence posts, we'd wish all our troubles were with Old Man Howe."

I had to agree with that. "So all we got is science."

"Okay. We can try science."

He hardly got the words out when two little meteors came ripping across the sky — and right behind them a big bright ball of fire. It looked like the big one was chasing the little ones, like there would be an explosion, but I knew there wouldn't be — they were too far away from each other.

It was hard to imagine those three pieces of dirt sitting there in space for maybe a million years, just waiting for the perfect moment — right when Arthur and I were watching. It was hard not to figure somebody had planned it. And it was hard not to make a wish, even if it was just to yourself.

When I looked back at Arthur, he had his eyes closed and was whispering something in Blackfoot.

I didn't know much of his language, but I knew this one — Arthur had told me once that they were the words of Big Lodge Pole, an old Blackfoot who died many years ago. Arthur said these words a lot. They meant "Make my enemy brave and strong, so that if defeated, I will not be ashamed."

The Rules of Shame

Arthur talked about Catface, how he didn't have a mom or dad like the other kids had, and how he'd been raised by the Fathers and Sisters and supervisors at Heavy Shield School. He wasn't even really a kid anymore, he was fourteen or maybe even fifteen. Anyway, Arthur said the kids called Catface the supervisors' baby because he was always with them and never had to do work like the other kids. So nobody liked him.

"Then why do you care about him now?" I asked. "Why don't we just give Howe back his papers?"

"Because Catface is an Indian."

I knew where this one was headed: Indians against white people, just like it had been for a hundred years. I didn't fight it.

We spent the next while trying to figure out Catface with science.

"Were Catface's mom and dad killed by some disease?" I asked. "And that's why he was raised by white people at Heavy Shield School?"

"I don't know."

"Why is he always so friendly with the supervisors?"

"I don't know."

"Do they like him more than the rest of the kids?"

"I don't know."

"Maybe they were afraid he'd tell all the secrets he knew about Heavy Shield School if they let him go."

"I don't know."

I gave Arthur a sour look. "Don't you understand how to figure something out with science?"

"Sure," Arthur said. "You ask me questions I don't know nothing about, and I say I don't know."

I gave Arthur a hard elbow in the ribs.

"Ouch," he said.

"How did that feel?"

"I don't know."

Once we finished rolling around on the ground and wrestling all over the blanket and Arthur got me in a leghold, I gave in and said, "Okay, science doesn't work on people."

After we got our wind back, we decided to wait until daylight and get a clue from the papers. Then we went back to watching the northeast sky.

At about three o'clock, the meteor shower ended. All it took was a single hour for the whole Earth to pass through the sand and ice and rocks of a million-year-old comet tail. I was all wished out, even if I didn't tell Arthur a single one.

Just as our eyelids were getting heavy, I asked Arthur, "Do you figure I'm strong enough to beat you in a real fight?"

"Not a real one."

"What if I was sneaky and hit you with a stick when your back was turned?"

"Then I'd feel like a fool for trusting you."

"You wouldn't feel ashamed?"

"That's stupid. We're friends. Friends don't ambush each other."

"I was just asking," I said, and rolled over.

Before I fell asleep, I wondered what Mr. Howe would feel if Catface beat him and his men — if he'd feel ashamed to be defeated by somebody weak. I wondered if Howe felt Arthur's rules of shame — the ones Arthur learned from Big Lodge Pole. I didn't think so, because Howe enjoyed stepping on people below him. If he didn't feel ashamed of that, there couldn't be much he'd feel ashamed of.

It's Worth Money

We woke to the sound of Arthur's mom chopping wood. The sun was sitting at about six o'clock. The moon was close behind. It wasn't new anymore — the first thin crescent moon would start tonight.

The ax hit.

Two pieces of wood stood for a second. One fell over, but the other one got split again before it could hit the ground. Arthur's mom is a pretty good chopper.

She picked up an armload of wood, stacked some kindling on top, and asked, "Make lots of wishes?"

"Oh, Mom," Arthur said. "Wishing is superstition."

"Wishing is for the heart," she said.

"I wished for bannock," I said.

"That was a very good wish," she said, and hauled the armload of wood into the house.

Arthur unfolded the papers, and in a second, we were going through them.

From inside the house came the smell of bannock frying and coffee bubbling.

"Darn," Arthur said. "No money in the daylight either."

"Not even on the back of the pages?"

"No place."

We wouldn't have taken the money — it just would've made it easier to figure out why the papers were so important. Instead, we had to go over every word to make sense of it.

"What's a Land Titles Office?" Arthur asked.

"I don't know."

"What's a Deed of Land?"

"I don't know."

"Who's Wilfred Black?"

"I don't know that either."

"Boy," Arthur said, "you're not very good at science."

"It's a government paper. You can't apply science to government."

We read the pages the best we could. They were written in some strange language. Most sentences started with "Whereas" or "The party of the first part" or "The power of The Court" and sometimes "The Province of Alberta."

"It sounds like a treaty," I said.

"Then we know it's worthless."

On the third from last page, we finally saw something interesting. It was an agreement between two men — their signatures were there, and so was the date they had signed it. "Mr. Clarence Howe" was printed in nice big letters, and beside it was Howe's rough-looking signature. Below "Mr. Clarence Howe" was the name "Wilfred Black" and beside it was an "X." The date said March 9, 1917.

Thirty-five years ago.

The last page was mostly blank except for a few lines at the top and a government seal on the bottom.

But the second from last page was the best of all. It was a map that showed the railway tracks and Grayson and a boundary drawing of a quarter section of land east of town.

Arthur looked at me with his eyes all bugged out.

"What?" I asked.

"That's a chunk of Howe's farm. And this piece of paper shows who owns the land."

"Wilfred Black?" I said, like I was answering a question.

"The man who signs his name with an X."

"This paper's worth money."

"Plenty."

The door bumped open behind us.

We turned with a nervous jerk, hiding the papers between our bodies and trying to look as innocent as possible.

Arthur's mom stood in the open door. She had flour on her hands and a nice smile on her face.

It was time for bannock.

He Looked Like He'd Seen a Ghost

Arthur and I sat as his mom put out the fried deer meat and bannock. When she returned to the cookstove to move the cast-iron frying pan off the heat and get the coffee, Arthur motioned to the table.

It was big with a shiny yellow top. The chairs had chrome legs with soft seats and padded armrests. Everything a person would ever need for eating was on the table: strawberry jam, sugar, canned milk and great big tin cups for coffee or tea.

Arthur gave me a little nudge.

"Gee," I said, rubbing my hands over the table, "this sure is a nice table."

"It's new," Arthur's mom said with a wide smile.

Arthur gave me another nudge. It meant thank you.

I'd already heard about the table. Arthur had told me his mom didn't like the white people's world much, but she sure liked tables and chairs. I had already known that. Once, she'd said she could allow a table and chairs into her house and maybe one white person, then she gave me a smile. I guess she'd meant me. She was quite a kidder.

We were just about to start eating when Arthur's grandpa crawled out from under a pile of blankets in the corner.

We put our food down and waited for him to get to his chair. There was some kind of Indian law that said the oldest person gets to eat first. I was just hoping he wouldn't take any of my food. Taking my food was his favorite joke.

Arthur's grandpa came around the table from behind me. He yawned and stretched and scratched his rear end.

I was starting to sweat.

He put his big brown hand on my shoulder, took a hard grip, and leaned forward. With his other hand, he reached around and made like he was going to snatch my bannock. Then he turned away and went to his chair really slowly. It took a while before he sat down at the table, too, and then he moved his food around like he was trying to decide what to eat first.

All the while, he was watching me.

Arthur's mom said something in Blackfoot.

He made a sign I'd seen before. It meant white people are foolish. Then he started to eat.

Arthur's mom sighed. "Would you pass the milk please?"

Arthur and I relayed the milk.

"Would you pass the strawberry jam please?"

We relayed the jam.

Arthur's grandpa made the foolish sign again, then he piled a bunch more food on his plate and got up from his chair.

He was awfully big. Arthur once told me that when his grandpa came to live with them, his dad had to make the door bigger so the old man could fit through without knocking the house down.

He walked past the cookstove and onto the blankets he'd been sleeping under.

His long gray hair hung loose around his shoulders, half hiding his face. His dark eyes were always on me, as if he saw something in me that even I couldn't see.

We all ate in peace for a while. Every now and then, I would look around the house. I was still a little nervous that maybe there was a grandma under those blankets, and that she'd crawl out and we'd all have to stop eating. But I knew there wasn't. She was buried behind the house.

The house was really just a room. And the table and chairs were the only furniture, unless you counted the cookstove and the piles of blankets, which went around the walls, where everybody slept. There was an extra big pile for Arthur's mom and dad.

"Where's your dad?" I whispered to Arthur.

"Working for Old Man Howe."

"Would you pass the sugar please?" Arthur's mom asked.

We relayed the sugar.

"Hauling grain?" I whispered to Arthur.

"Paying for a table and chairs."

Arthur's mom was looking at us. "It's not polite to whisper at the table."

"We were talking about how nice it looks," Arthur said.

She made a little smile.

Arthur gave me a nudge.

"Sure is a nice table," I said. "And the chairs are about as soft as I've ever seen in my life."

That got me a second helping of everything. After I let out a polite burp, I started thinking about the deed. That quarter section really wasn't much more than a small piece of Howe's farm. After all, his whole place was more than ten sections.

I took a gulp of coffee and thought about Wilfred Black. Usually a name will bring a face with it if you leave it long enough, but it wasn't coming with Wilfred Black. I wondered who he was. Maybe he was dead by now. If he wasn't dead, he'd be awfully old.

It was about then that Arthur pointed to the papers hidden under his shirt. He motioned his head toward his grandpa. Then, when his mom wasn't looking, he mouthed the words "Wilfred Black."

I gave him a confused look.

He gave me another nudge.

"Oh," I said. It came out before I knew it. But I understood.

I glanced at Arthur's mom, then at his grandpa.

Arthur kicked me under the table.

I swallowed the last of my coffee. "I saw Wilfred Black yesterday," I said, and looked at Arthur's mom.

She had her hands folded in her lap. She looked thoughtful and polite. I guess the name was new to her too.

Then I looked at Arthur's grandpa.

He looked like he'd seen a ghost.

"I was walking along the tracks," I said. "East of town. I saw Mr. Black hanging around on Howe's land."

Arthur looked quickly back and forth between his mom and his grandpa. I guessed I was headed in the right direction.

"He was a little tired out from his long walk," I said. "Being kind of old and all, but he was happy to be back in Grayson just the same."

Arthur's mom was still looking thoughtful and listening.

Arthur's face was red, like he'd stopped breathing.

Arthur's grandpa stared at me for a few long seconds. Then he came right up to me, put one hand on my armrest, and bent over, his mouth close to my ear. His breath was hot against my skin, and in it I could hear his low, harsh words. "Don't bring shame on this house, foolish white boy." He straightened up and put both his hands on my shoulders, close to my neck.

Ever since the first day I saw Arthur's grandpa, I figured he was nearly a hundred. Now he closed his grip so tight my breath stopped in my chest, and I knew there was more to him than years. And I knew he could hurt me if he wanted to.

Arthur and his mom were looking at us.

I knew a warning when I got one.

No Better than Indians

Arthur and I took the last page from the deed, the one that was mostly blank except for the few lines at the top and the Province of Alberta seal on the bottom, and headed to the post office. Hanging inside was a government handbill asking young men to join the army and fight the Communists in Korea.

I pushed the door open and stepped inside. The room was empty except for the wall of mailboxes and a counter with a glass top, some pencils and a fountain pen. The only sound came from behind the closed wicket, where the postmaster was sliding boxes across the floor and opening and closing doors as he got ready for his day.

The big clock above the wicket said fifteen minutes to eight o'clock.

I tiptoed to the counter.

"Hurry up," Arthur whispered, looking at the clock.

I unfolded the deed page, pressed it flat on the glass counter, and picked up a pencil.

Arthur shook his head. "Use the pen. A pencil will look like a kid made it."

I took the fountain pen from beside the inkwell.

The postmaster slammed a door.

I jumped. That gave the pen a quick jerk and flipped a line of ink up the wall.

Arthur glanced over my shoulder. "Careful. Inky paper will look like a fool made the bill."

"Do you want me to hurry? Or do you want me to be careful?"

"Both," he said, and gave me the shush sign.

I started to print using straight, dark lines.

"Make 'farm' in big letters."

I had to stick my tongue out the side of my mouth just to get the letters straight. I had to chew on it to make "farm" the way Arthur said.

"Sign it with an X," he whispered.

There goes my tongue, I thought as I finished the X. "How's that?"

"Good."

We blew on the ink until it was dry. Then Arthur took the paper to the billboard, half covered the government bill, pulled out the government tack, and stuck it through both papers.

We stepped back and put our hands on our hips.

Our bill covered the government bill except for the word "fight." That made it look like the word was part of our bill.

Arthur went to tack it in a better spot, but I shook my head when I saw how the words lined up:

> *Fight*
> *Wilfred Black*
> *He*
> *has come for his*
> *FARM*
> X

Below all that was the Alberta government seal.

"'Farm' stands out pretty good," Arthur said.

"People will think of 'farm' when they read Wilfred Black's name."

I expect that was what Arthur wanted.

The word "fight" made it seem as if the government was in on Wilfred Black's land deal. The X made it look like Wilfred Black himself had signed it. And the government seal made it all very official.

With any luck, it would rile up the town people and get them talking and maybe even arguing, then Arthur and I could just hang around and listen. It was pretty sneaky, but we figured nobody in town would just tell two kids about Mr. Howe's secret business, even if they knew about it.

Arthur pushed the tack in good and deep and we snuck out of the post office before the postmaster opened the little wicket door and saw us fooling around with the tack and the billboard. There was probably a law against moving government tacks.

We leaned against the east-facing wall and took a big breath. To our right was the outside billboard, where people hung bills when the post office was closed. There, a Korea bill hung, its edges already curled up in the sun, and it was barely eight o'clock. It was going to be one really hot prairie day.

Arthur brushed his hands together like he'd finished a dirty job. "Okay. Let's go talk to Catface."

We crossed Main Street to Frankie's store and headed up Grierson Street, past the row of big poplars, turned right at the lumber yard and headed for the jail. We figured that was a good place to start looking. Along the way, I told Arthur that his grandpa had called me a foolish white boy.

"He calls me a foolish redskin."

"Yeah, but he said it after I said Wilfred Black's name."

We passed the tall fence around the lumber yard. The air smelled like freshly cut wood.

"He knows Wilfred Black," Arthur said.

I shook my head. "If my grandpa was alive, he'd'a told me everything about Wilfred Black, if he knew anything."

"Don't expect that from my grandpa."

Rows of split cedar fence posts lined the near side of the lumber yard.

"Is he too old to remember good?" I asked.

Arthur stopped where a big stack of posts reached above the fence. "Grandpa rode with Heavy Shield and Red Crow and Old Sun and Crowfoot and even Lame Bull in Montana."

"So?"

Arthur gave me the foolish sign.

"What was that for?"

"You don't understand Indians."

"Sure I do. I know your grandpa won't tell us about Wilfred Black because he's too stubborn."

Arthur laughed. "He's not telling us anything, because he thinks we're not old enough to be treated like anything but kids."

"How about if we were as old as Catface? Would he tell us then?"

"He might not ever tell us."

"I guess you're right — I don't know much about Indians."

When I looked back at Arthur, his eyes were bright, like he knew something I would never understand.

"Let's go talk to Catface," he said, and slapped my arm.

At the end of the high fence, the scent of cedar had spilled out onto the sidewalk. It smelled like a whole forest had been cut down and stacked in the yard.

"Was it a stupid idea to make the bill?" I asked.

"No."

I gave a sigh of relief.

"It was stupid to put it up."

Oh brother, I thought.

I glanced at Arthur. He always looked like he was thinking, even when we weren't in some kind of trouble. He was thinking extra hard right now.

I agreed with Arthur about making the bill and putting it up. I knew it was a dangerous thing to do, but I also knew we wouldn't find out anything just by asking. Asking questions about Mr. Howe and Wilfred Black and the deed would have made people suspicious. And maybe Howe would have found out we had the deed.

Boy, there'd've been trouble then.

"Arthur, why do you think Catface stole the deed from Howe?"

"To get it away from him."

"That's like saying we're walking because we're going someplace."

"We're going someplace because of what Howe did."

"Because he beat up Catface?"

"No."

"What did Howe do if he didn't beat up Catface?"

"I believe he cheated this Black fellow, just like he cheats Indians any chance he gets."

"I don't want to talk about who Howe cheats."

"He cheats everybody. Maybe even his own family. Heck, Wilfred Black could be Howe's son."

"You're being stupid."

Arthur grinned.

"What's so funny?"

"Your family used to have a good deal more land," he said.

"That was a long time ago, when Grandpa was still alive."

Arthur stopped.

I walked past a step or two and stopped. Hearing those words made me think about Aunt Molly — how she'd died after we lost our land.

"Who's got that land now?" Arthur asked.

I turned and stared at him. His eyes looked like there was fire behind them.

"I can tell you, if you can't remember," Arthur said.

"We lost it. You want me to say the bank took it during the dust storms? So what if it did? I wasn't even born then." I didn't say anything about Aunt Molly. It was none of Arthur's business.

"Your family was too poor to keep that land and Howe was rich enough to buy it cheap from the bank. Indians get thrown in jail for stealing less than Howe stole from your family."

"I don't know nothing about Howe's business. Maybe Black cheated him and Howe is just getting back what is his."

"He cheated your family just like they were Indians."

My face got hot like it was on fire. "We're not Indians!" I hollered, before I could stop the heat.

Arthur walked right up to me, his face so close to mine we almost touched. "Howe doesn't see the difference. I'm poor and red and you're poor and white — that will only slow him down by half a step."

I started walking fast. For a second, I felt angry at Arthur for saying my family was no better than

Indians, and that made my stomach turn. I wished it didn't matter to me. I wished all the town talk never got into me. But it did. It was part of me, like my hair is brown and I'm poor. I felt ashamed of my mom and dad and brother and myself too — because we were no better than Indians.

Arthur caught up. "I don't mind if he believes there's no difference between us."

"I know," I said, and kept walking.

"You okay?"

"Sure."

We walked another half a block.

"I figure there's lots of Indians who know about Wilfred Black," Arthur said. "Other than Grandpa, I mean."

"Lots of town people too," I added. "Other than me, of course."

"It was a good idea to make the bill."

"We'll have to watch out for Sergeant Findley."

"He'll back Howe and the town people," Arthur said. "He'd never back a poor kid."

"Or an Indian kid," I said.

I wanted to tell Arthur that if things didn't work out, I'd go to jail with him and sit on the steel bench beside him. Instead, I walked on with my head down, angry at Grayson.

Spy Hill Was Full of Indians

We turned into a half-a-square-block of tall grass and old trees. It was going to be a kids' playground someday, so the town council had said, but it looked like a forest. Across the street was the Mountie barracks. In front was Sergeant Findley's car, with Mr. Howe's Fargo truck parked behind it.

We stopped in the poplar shadows and watched. Everything was still.

"I'll bet Howe beat Catface good before he had Findley lock him up," Arthur said.

"I expect Sergeant Findley is doing what he's told."

"Yeah. Which one's worse, the one who gives the orders or the one who does the dirty work?"

"Both, I guess." I looked through our cover of trees and tall grass. I couldn't see anyone moving behind the windows. "Do you figure Catface told on us?"

"I don't think so."

"Howe scares me," I said. "If I had to, I'd rather go up against Sergeant Findley."

Arthur made a sound like he was blowing out dirty air. "You just wait 'til Findley catches you when nobody's watching, or when it's night, or when he figures you're poor enough to be treated like an Indian."

I blew out my air like Arthur had done, only I didn't have anything to say about anything connected to it, so I just squinted at the Mountie barracks and made the sound again.

"We better talk to Catface before he gets shipped off to some real jail," I said.

"Or killed."

"Better get it all figured out today."

"No use wasting time when it comes to trouble."

I nodded. No use, I thought. But it was pretty early in the day. With any luck, we'd have it solved by noon.

Arthur peered through the trees. "You ready?"

"Sure."

We stepped back and worked our way through the grass and trees to the north edge of the playground. I stopped and held up my hand, then checked. It was clear. We turned east, crossed the street in front of the barracks, and headed down the alley to the small barred windows where the cells were.

Two Mountie cars were parked out back, beside the panel truck for rounding up drunk Indians. One Mountie car must have been out on patrol.

Two rows of scruffy-looking caragana hedges grew between the alley and the lawn and barracks. We slipped through a hole in the bushes, crouched low, and held up on the narrow path running between the hedges. In front of us, across the narrow strip of grass and high up the wall, were the barred windows. To the right was the back door to the Mountie barracks. It made me nervous because there wasn't any cover between us and the door.

For a moment longer, we watched the building. It was made of red brick set on a thick concrete foundation about five feet off the ground. On the foundation was a narrow ledge topped with concrete that sloped down at a sharp angle.

Arthur pointed to the far left corner. "We'll have to climb up to that ledge. Then shinny along it to the windows."

"If a fella was tall enough, he could grab the bars and look right inside the cells."

"You want to do it?" Arthur whispered.

"Why? You're taller than me. You scared?"

"No use both of us getting caught."

"Scared, huh?"

"Yeah. If I get caught, I'll be behind one of those little windows. If you get caught, you'll just get a bawling out and be sent home. Besides, even Old Man Howe would give you half a step head start over an Indian."

"Okay."

I slipped off my shoes and ran, half crouched, to the low corner, then I spit on my hands and wiped the bottoms of my feet. That would make my feet a little sticky and maybe keep me from slipping off and falling on my head. I crawled up to the ledge, gripped the space between the bricks kind of low with my fingertips, and pulled like I was lifting something heavy. That pushed down on my feet and gave me a good grip at both ends.

I shinnied along like that until I got to the first window. There, I grabbed hold of the sill and stood on tiptoe. Even with my face pushed between the bars, I could only see half the cell. The floor was about seven feet below the bars. The edge of an old mattress stuck out from the back wall. A short length of chain hung from the corners of the metal frame holding the bed to the wall.

Footsteps thumped down the long hallway.

I ducked just as a redheaded constable grabbed the barred door and shook it.

"Hey, redskin!" he called. "Checkout time at the crowbar hotel."

An old Indian voice grumbled about still being sleepy.

I moved to the next cell. A man was throwing up on the floor. When I got to the third window, a pair of hard hands grabbed the bars and a big dark face looked right at me.

I let out a small scream and ducked below the sill.

A low laugh came from the window, then a voice said, "Psst, white man. Got a smoke?" He reached out and poked my hand. "Hey, white man."

I looked up. His face was hard and square. Long black braids hung past his shoulders. He had dark, angry eyes. He held the bars with an easy grip, like his hands were used to being there.

I caught my breath and spoke as quietly as I could. "Did you see Catface?"

"What's a white man want with an Indian?"

"He's in trouble. Arthur and I are trying to help him." I looked over my shoulder and waved for Arthur to show himself.

Arthur stuck his head through the hole in the hedge and held up my shoes.

The man nodded at Arthur and mumbled something in Blackfoot, then stared at me. "All I ever see is Mounties." A braid fell across his face when he tipped his head toward the last cell. "Look there. I heard crying last night."

I said thanks and went to go.

"What about my smokes?"

"I don't smoke."

The last cell was empty. I slipped off the ledge, rolled in the grass to break my fall, and ran back to the caragana bush.

"Who is that man?" I asked as I pulled on my shoes.

"You wouldn't be able to pronounce his name," Arthur said. "But it means Lowhorn."

"He said he heard crying in the cell at the end. It's empty now."

"Maybe Sergeant Findley has a secret place for beating up prisoners."

That's when I heard Findley's voice from behind the back door.

Lowhorn was still standing on the mattress, looking out his little barred window. His hands had turned into veiny lumps on either side of his face. "Get outta here!" he called. "They're coming!"

Arthur and I backed into the hedge as the door flew open. Sergeant Findley came out dragging Catface down the stairs. Catface clawed and scratched at the door. Then he caught hold of the steel handrail and held on. Findley jerked him hard. Catface's grip broke, and he landed at Findley's feet.

"Quit fighting, you little son of a —" Findley said.

A second later, something bumped into the bushes and tried to push me through the hole in the hedge. I looked over my shoulder as the Mountie car stopped and the engine died.

"Jeez," Arthur whispered.

We dropped to the ground and wiggled backward under the bumper. The on-patrol constable stepped out and stood between his car and the panel truck. I held my breath and looked at his boots. They were big and black and shiny.

"Do you need a hand over there, Sergeant?" he called to Findley.

Arthur ran his hand across his forehead and mouthed "Boy, that was close."

Then Lowhorn started hollering. He grabbed the bars and pushed his face at a sharp angle. He stuck his arm clear out and slapped the sole of a shoe against the bricks. It sounded like there were ten men in his cell, all fighting about something.

He hollered at Catface in Blackfoot.

Catface called back and tried to stand.

Findley stepped on his hand.

Catface screamed.

Lowhorn cussed and spit at Findley. And when he saw the on-patrol constable, he hollered something pretty mean about the constable's grandmother and mother and sister and daughter.

I didn't believe the constable was married, so he wouldn't have a daughter. But he got mad just the same.

Catface jerked his hand out from under Sergeant Findley's foot. He got two steps and fell over his own feet. Findley took one easy step and twisted his boot against Catface's bare ankle, like he was squashing a cigarette butt.

"Constable!" Findley called. "Take this prisoner back to his cell. I've got some business to attend to."

While the on-patrol constable pushed Catface back inside the building, Sergeant Findley walked out into the alley and stood tapping the black billy against his boot top, his big bald head shiny with sweat in the morning sun.

Beside me, Arthur was praying. It didn't help. In a few seconds, Findley was standing beside the driver's door. He moved some gravel around with his foot, then flipped the pile right into my face.

"Get out from under this car," he ordered.

Arthur went to crawl out. I shook my head and pointed to the hole in the hedge.

"Whud I tell you?" Findley said.

I worked my way to where Findley was standing, felt for the car's frame with my feet, then gave a hard shove. My shoulders hit his boots with a thump. He landed on his rear end. A cloud of dust shot into the air.

"What in damnation do you think you're doing?"

"Sorry, Sergeant," I said, rubbing my eyes. "I couldn't see where I was going with all that dirt in my face."

By the time Sergeant Findley was finished cussing me and we were both standing, Arthur was through the hole in the caragana bushes and had disappeared around the corner of the barracks.

"Where's the other one?"

"What other one?"

"That Indian you're always hanging around with."

"I expect he's at home."

Findley bent over and looked under the car. "What were you fooling with under this car? You planning on draining the oil and having a constable seize up an engine?"

I stared at him.

"What's wrong with you?"

"You got me clean on this one, Sergeant. I'd've done it, too, if I hadn't lost my crescent wrench someplace."

"You're one dumb kid, Samson. Your brains must have turned to mush trying to learn that redskin language." He brushed the dirt off his pants. "Jeez. Not even enough sense to lie."

I said something in Blackfoot.

"What did you say?"

"Aren't you going to throw me in jail?"

"Get out of my sight."

"Okay. But I'll have to come back later and find my wrench."

"I don't believe it," he said, shaking his head. "You're more Indian every day."

I snickered as I walked up the alley and turned down the street to the future playground.

"Psst," Arthur said as I passed.

I ducked into the trees and knelt beside him.

"What happened with Findley? I didn't expect you'd get away so easy."

"I acted dumb."

"And he let you go?"

"Not exactly," I said. "I had to promise not to drain the oil outta any more Mountie cars 'til their oil change was due."

Arthur was still shaking his head when Howe walked out the front door of the barracks, climbed into his truck, and headed toward downtown. A few seconds later, the Mountie panel truck came around the corner, too. Sergeant Findley was driving and Kratz, the supervisor from Heavy Shield School, was sitting beside him. In the back, Catface looked out the glass-and-cage-wire window. He was quite a mess.

"Darn," Arthur said. "They're taking him to Spy Hill."

Spy Hill is a jail near Calgary. It's full of Indians.

"We can't follow him there," I said.

"We'll have to figure this out without Catface's help."

"It's a good thing we put up the bill in the post office."

"Howe is probably there right now, reading it," Arthur said, and grinned.

We waited until everything was quiet again, then we snuck back around to Lowhorn's cell and threw rocks at the bars. It took a long time before he looked out. When he did, I almost cried from how he looked. One eye was purple and swollen shut, and his lip looked like he had a whole can of snuff stuffed under it.

He gave Arthur a quick nod and dropped out of sight.

We walked down the alley toward the railway tracks. As we went, Arthur kicked rocks and tin cans. Then he started cussing the constables and Sergeant

Findley. By the time we'd got a full block, he had worked his way all the way back to cussing Treaty Number 7. And that happened in 1877.

It took a while before Arthur calmed down and even longer before he caught his breath. Cussing can be awful hard work.

"What do you figure Lowhorn did to get thrown in jail?" I asked.

"Something pretty bad," Arthur said. "Maybe he spit on the street or said good morning to a white woman."

"That's stupid. He probably got drunk."

"Like your dad."

"My dad's never been in jail."

"But he's been drunk plenty of times."

"That's different. Dad doesn't get into fights when he's drinking."

Arthur shook his head. "You've a ways to go before you know enough to be an Indian."

"I know plenty now. I know what it's like to be an Indian."

"You're just a foolish white boy."

Things never changed in Grayson. Sergeant Findley and Howe could do whatever they liked. Poor people didn't matter. And Indians mattered even less. I felt a little bit hopeless. But Arthur wasn't hopeless. He'd got over that a hundred years ago. Now he was just mad.

I pointed at a Spam tin.

Arthur wound up and kicked it.

It made a high curve, sailed over a fence into a backyard and landed, rattling on a concrete sidewalk.

"Hey," a fat man called from the yard, "you stupid kids!"

"Fatso," Arthur called back.

"Come on," I said. "We've got a mystery to solve."

We headed down the alley.

Behind us the fat man grumbled, "I might'a guessed, Indians."

Arthur stopped halfway down the next block, pulled out the map from the deed, and looked at it. The rest of the deed was hidden in Arthur's woodpile. He poked at Wilfred Black's quarter section.

"Let's take a look at this important piece of land," he said.

"It's just a field. What can we figure out by looking at a grain field?"

"Remember that old boxcar sitting on the edge of the trees?"

"Sure."

"Somebody lived there once."

"It's full of garbage. Besides, it's on Mrs. Bowman's land, not Howe's."

"No. It's on this quarter." He turned the map so I could see.

"Okay, if you say so," I said, then added, "but what if Howe's there looking for Wilfred Black?"

"That's what I'm hoping," Arthur said. "And if he is, most likely Loewan'll be there, too, and Loewan talks a pretty good story."

"Dad said it's just the beer talking. But I expect he'll be puttin' on the big-shot act if there's hired men to brag to."

"Good," Arthur said. He folded the map and slipped it into his hip pocket.

As we walked down the alley, I thought about our bill hanging in the post office. But instead of Wilfred Black's X, my name was there in big bold letters. It gave me an awful shiver to think what Mr. Howe would do if he found out it was me who'd made the bill and Arthur who'd hung it on the billboard.

The Old Lady in the Woods

We headed to the south edge of town and turned east where the railway tracks crossed the road joining the reserve to the main highway. In twenty minutes, we crossed the irrigation ditch that flowed under the tracks, past the remains of Kratz's coal-oil lantern, the burned railway ties and Catface's charred shirt. After another hour we passed Mrs. Bowman's fields, stopped at a bluff, and stared at the old boxcar sitting on railway ties on the edge of her property.

"See? Isn't that what I said?"

"Okay, so it's on Bowman's land," Arthur said.

"Well, would you look at Howe's grain," I said. "If that isn't the most suspicious-looking wheat I ever saw."

"Don't be so smart."

Arthur held the map out and looked back toward Mrs. Bowman's house, comparing the map to the land in front of us. He scratched his head and looked east, away from Grayson.

"You lost?" I asked.

"Pretty hard to get turned around when you're following a railway track."

After a minute of considering the map, Arthur handed it to me. "Where's Mrs. Bowman's house on this thing?"

"It's not here," I said. "This map was made in 1917. There was no house."

"Show me the irrigation ditch."

I pointed to the map.

Arthur shook his head. "It wasn't there in 1917 either."

"What's that then?"

"Buffalo Creek."

We'd read the map wrong. Howe's land was on the other side of Buffalo Creek. I guess getting it wrong wasn't our fault — Howe had land all over the county — but I still felt discouraged.

"That's another four miles. We can't go that far."

"Come on," Arthur said, and started taking long, fast steps that covered three ties at a time.

"Wait up!" I called. "How do you know there's anything there but fields?"

"I've got a feeling."

"I'm already tired."

"Well, stay here and wait for me."

"Why is it that my feelings are always wrong?" I called as I ran to catch up. "And yours are always right?"

"Siksika know how to listen."

"Siksika" is what the Blackfoot call themselves. I didn't believe that Arthur had better feelings about things than I did. He was just better at guessing.

I had a big grin on my face.

"I know what you're thinking," Arthur said.

"Your feelings were wrong about the boxcar."

"No, they weren't. I just shouldn't have trusted a white man's map."

Oh brother, I thought.

We crossed Buffalo Creek and walked east another two miles. There were no roads or houses, and the main highway to the north was so far away that we couldn't even hear the big trucks.

In another half hour, we were sitting on the railway tracks with the map resting on the ground between us. Arthur set a stone on each corner and looked out at the land in front of us. The field went north a quarter of a mile and east a full mile, just like the map showed. The wheat was tall and thick. Grain fields stretched out for miles in every direction — except for behind us, of course. That was the Indian reserve.

The breeze lifted one corner of the map and the stone rolled to the middle. Arthur moved his foot to that corner and held the map still.

I was so worn out I didn't care that Arthur's feelings had been wrong again.

In front of us, the wheat rolled like a green prairie sea. I felt sleepy, like it was night again, and Arthur and I were fighting to stay awake so we wouldn't miss the meteor shower.

Last year, Mr. Parks told our class that the ocean was the best place in the whole world to see the stars from. I wondered what it would feel like to float on a sea of wheat, with a million grassy fingertips tickling my back as I looked up at stars all the way back to forever.

Arthur stood with his back to the reserve, its crop of sunburned prairie grass stiff in the moving air. He glanced east, then west to the big poplar woods on our left.

"This is the spot," he said, as if he expected Wilfred Black to step out of the woods and wave us on in.

I leaned back on my elbows, half closed my eyes, and let the breeze blow across my face as I watched the waves.

"Nice grain," I said softly.

"Nice for Howe."

"Sure. But I figure Wilfred Black would like it just the same. Who do you suppose he is?"

"Just another man cheated by Howe."

I watched a green wave of wheat crash onto the pile of rocks that held the tracks, and went off into a sleepy daydream. Arthur's talking was just low mumbles mixed with the sound of the wind and the waves and a far-off train whistle.

Arthur pushed me with his foot. "I said, someone's chopping wood."

"Chopping?"

"Over in the poplar woods." He gave me a cross look and pulled me up by the arm. "Let's get outta sight."

Whack, came the sound of the ax.

We stumbled down the reserve side of the tracks, bent over, and ran quietly on toward the sound. Across from the woods, we crawled back up the mound of rocks and looked over the rails. There was nothing to see except trees. We slid over the tracks and snuck into the woods. Along the near edge grew thick poplar suckers five to ten feet high and about six inches apart. Past them, the trees were twenty feet high, with almost enough space between them for us to crawl without having to wiggle.

It was awfully tough going.

Farther into the woods, the suckers and small trees gave way to bigger ones, then to old trees about four to six feet around and seventy feet high.

The sound of the ax cracked through the woods.

Arthur dropped to the ground like he'd been shot.

I dropped beside him.

"Did you see anything?" Arthur asked.

"No."

"Figure the sound came from the left?"

"At worst, straight ahead."

"Good," Arthur said, motioning to the right. "Let's work our way around those two big trees and come up on the ax from the other side."

I had just rolled over when something rustled in the grass behind us.

"Jeez, Arthur. Something's following us."

"Let's get outta here."

We got to our hands and knees and scrambled away from the rustling sound, back toward the densely growing poplar.

The rustling grew louder.

"Faster," Arthur said.

I looked up in time to see the ax cut through the air and then land, driven clear out of sight, into the ground right in front of my face. The steel made a cool wind as it brushed past my nose. From behind us came an awful growl. A large black dog burst through the grass and jumped.

Arthur rolled into the underbrush and disappeared.

The dog hit my back with all fours, sliding my shirt up to my neck. I twisted under his weight, got onto my back, and crossed my arms over my face. His jowls dripped strings of foamy spit. He smelled of rotting flesh. For a second, he was still, like he was waiting for something. I didn't wait to find out what it was. I pulled my knee up and drove it into the base of his ribs.

He let out an "oof" sound and bit at me.

"Down, dog!" hollered a rough voice.

I ripped my shirt from his teeth. The ax jerked from the damp ground, bringing up a piece of half-rotten wood and some of last fall's leaves. The sun caught the steel and flashed in my eyes as the ax swung past the dog's neck. He was in mid-bite when the ax hit the ground again, just missing my arm. The dog's head snapped back, and he made a choking growl.

A second later, Arthur jumped from the underbrush, swinging a heavy poplar branch. "I'll kill it!" he screamed. "Get a hold of that dog or I'll kill it!"

An Indian woman stood over me. Her hair was short and black, her face round and pockmarked. She grabbed the ax handle in a tight grip. Then she reached down in the leaves and grabbed a thick rope that had been shoved deep in the dirt by the blade. She stood there for a few seconds, looking between Arthur and me.

"Keep that branch still or you'll be the one getting killed," she said, and jerked the ax from the ground.

She ran her hand down the side of the dog's wide head and patted his neck. When I tried to crawl away, she kicked me so hard in the rear end that, if I hadn't fallen on my face, I would've come right up to standing.

Arthur got a two-handed grip on the poplar branch. Its leaves trembled.

She held the ax like it was a little stick and pointed the blade toward the tracks. "Drop my firewood. And get outta here."

The dog gave me a quick bark.

We backed up slowly, keeping a close eye on the dog and the ax. Behind us, the steel wheels of the train clacked slowly over the rails.

Deeper into the woods, half hidden in the old poplars, we could just see an overgrown cabin. An old woman stood with her head sticking out the door.

"Who's there, Alice?" she asked as she came out.

"Get inside," the pockfaced woman said.

"I want to see them."

"Get inside and shut the door, or I'll put the dog on you."

The old woman didn't listen. Instead, she walked through a little clearing between us and the shack, looked at me, then at Arthur standing in the tall grass. She had a big smile when she said, "A reserve boy. I like reserve —" She didn't finish. She just turned a gray color, and her mouth opened. "Willy?" she whispered to Arthur. "Don't you recognize me? It's Emmy. Your —"

"Shut up," Pockface said.

Arthur glanced from the old woman to me, then shrugged.

The old woman was wearing a long nightdress that was dirty from the bottom all the way to her knees. I got a funny feeling all over my body when she called herself Emmy, and when I saw those pale-blue eyes that looked somewhere between ice and the clear summer sky over my head, I knew she was somebody I knew.

I had seen her late one night when I was little and got lost in my own yard looking for our outhouse. As Old Man Howe's truck passed our lane, I saw somebody sitting beside him. In a second, the truck door flew open and a woman jumped out and knocked me over as I ran. She looked down at me with those eyes and the same scared-to-death gray color she was now. Then Old Man Howe grabbed her by the arm and dragged her back to the truck.

I'd thought she looked like a dead person, but I was wrong — she was just crazy. Everybody in Grayson knew her from rumors. Most people thought she'd died, but some said she was locked up in the Ponoka insane hospital. I remember telling Dad about what I'd seen. He strapped me for lying. I forgot about her in a hurry after that. Until now.

I figured I was the only person who had ever really seen her. Now Arthur had, too.

She was Old Man Howe's crazy daughter, Emma.

The Indian woman gave the dog a little kick, and it let out a bunch of barks and growls as it jerked on the heavy rope.

Arthur and I ran for the tracks.

"Please, Alice," Emma Howe begged.

"You crazy old fool," Pockface said. "He's not Willy."

Behind us came an awful, sorrowful sound. Emma Howe was crying like a little girl.

Crazy Emma's Lovey

Arthur ran straight into the poplar suckers. The deeper he went, the more tangled he got. I was smaller, so I could wiggle my way to where the suckers were small enough to push over.

I burst out of the woods and almost ran into the freight train stopped on the tracks.

Arthur thrashed and cussed, then screamed like he was attacking something. A tree broke with a loud crack. Arthur whooped, and a few seconds later he ripped past me and beside the tracks, next to the train.

Leaves and bits of branches stuck out from his hair and pockets and buttonholes and even his belt loops. He looked like a tree with legs — with a map flapping in its back pocket.

I was falling behind pretty fast.

"Hold up, Willy!" I hollered.

Arthur gave me a backhand wave. A handful of leaves spun in the wind and settled over the rock slope.

"Crazy Emma's Willy!"

Arthur put his hands over his ears and kept running.

"Oh, Willy Howe."

I shouldn't have said that. I knew Arthur didn't like Mr. Howe — he maybe even hated him. So it was pretty stupid to make it sound like he was related to Mr. Howe.

Arthur stopped and glared. His eyes were red, and his nostrils flared like a wild man's.

I let out an "Oh boy" and stopped far enough away that he couldn't hit me.

Arthur caught his breath. "Is it the white man's job to shame an Indian whenever he gets a chance?"

"Jeez, Arthur, it was just a joke."

"You think Indians are funny?"

Arthur walked back to me as the train started to move. When the cars banged one against the other, I jumped. He must have thought I was going to run because he grabbed me by the shirt and jerked me toward him.

I should have been scared, but Arthur looked so funny with leaves and little branches sticking out all over the place that I grinned right at him, then snickered.

"You think *I'm* funny?"

"No," I said.

"Howe cheated your family just like they were Indians," Arthur said, using the same words that had got me so mad in town.

My face got hot as fire. I didn't say anything, but I lost my smirk in a big hurry.

"I'm sorry," I said. "It's just that you look like you're in disguise as a tree. You're not Willy Howe."

Arthur let go of my shirt and brushed the leaves from his hair. "Besides," he said over the clack of the train wheels, "*your* name is Willy, not mine."

"Yeah. Well, so is Wilfred Black's, if you say it like his mom is talking." I glanced at the train. When I looked back, Arthur had gone all pale. "What?" I asked.

"Wilfred Black," Arthur said, then paused for a long time. "*He's* Emma Howe's Willy."

I got an awful shiver, like somebody was walking over my grave. I thought about the bill hanging in the post office, and that we had been seen on Howe's land by Emma Howe and the pockfaced woman. They could easily describe us to Mr. Howe. I was the only white kid who had an Indian friend. We would get into big trouble when Mr. Howe heard we were snooping around on his land the day that the handbill showed up in the post office.

Now I agreed with Arthur's grandpa. I was foolish. And Howe wasn't. He had to be pretty smart to get so rich. Soon enough he would figure out it was Arthur and me who put up the bill. It was also too late to change getting seen by Emma Howe and the pockfaced woman. But it wasn't too late for something else.

I swallowed hard. "We gotta get that bill back before Howe reads it."

"I know."

We stood looking west, where Grayson was just a small dot, as the boxcars slowly picked up speed. In a second, we were both running as if we had one mind with one idea.

Arthur grabbed the metal ladder that hung from the back of the grain car and pulled himself up. Before he got to the top, I was halfway up the ladder. At the back of the train, the caboose man was hollering and shaking his fist.

Ship 'Em to Korea

Arthur and I worked our way along the top of the boxcars until we got to the engine. The wind was blowing hard now that the train had a good head of steam. It looked like it wouldn't stop until we reached Calgary.

Arthur pointed to the sewage pond between the tracks and the road coming into Grayson. "Get to the ladder. We'll have to jump."

"In that stuff?" I called back.

"You'd rather jump on a pile of rocks?"

We stood just in time to see Joe Backfat head his horse and wagon over the road crossing. The horse was deaf and Joe was usually so drunk he might as well've been. Arthur jerked me down, and we grabbed hold of the roof frame of the grain car. The wheels locked and screamed against the rails, the whistle howling as a cloud of steam rolled across the cars. The train slid right through the crossing before it stopped. When Arthur and I looked up, the old horse was looking straight ahead, walking up the road. Joe's chin was resting on his chest — sound asleep. Just as well he didn't hear what the engineer was hollering at him.

"Joe's always had a lucky streak," Arthur said, and he jumped from the ladder.

"The horse is fair lucky himself."

We veered off the railway tracks, crossed over the station platform, and headed down the sidewalk beside the post office to the shallow lean-to roof protecting the outside billboard. Arthur glanced at the Korea bill hanging all alone with its edges curled up from getting rained on, then baked by the sun. A smear of bird poop had run down the soldier's face and dried in a lump on his rifle butt.

"Whud'e'ya figure that little roof is for?" I asked.

"Gives the pigeons a place to shoot from."

"Pretty good shots," I said, wiping the sweat off my face. "Maybe we should'a put our bill out here."

Arthur gave me a look.

"What was that for?"

"You agreed on it being a good idea to hang it in the post office."

"Yeah. But I figured you'd argue about it like you always do, so I just gave in."

"I don't always argue," Arthur argued.

"Yes you do."

I could tell Arthur was working up to a good "Oh yeah?" when the post-office door banged open and a group of men stomped out into the street, talking in rough voices that were mostly cussing. About a dozen men milled around the door.

"Holy smoke," one man said.

"Darn me to the fiery pit and back again," another one said.

"Well, I'll be a monkey's uncle," still another said.

Arthur gave me the shush sign, and we shuffled among the men, stuffed our hands in our pockets, and slouched around like they were doing.

"Son of a gun," Arthur said, and spit on the ground.

"Holy, darn it to the fiery pit, if I ain't a close relation to a monkey," I said.

The men looked at the ground where Arthur had spit, then up at me. I spit, too. Pretty soon we were all cussing back and forth and spitting.

Mr. Clarkson pulled up the bottom of his butcher's apron and wiped his hands. When he let go, the apron stayed rough and lumpy, held there by days of dried blood. The air smelled like sawdust and meat from his butcher shop. He grabbed our bill from a farmhand and stared at it.

"Well, sell me a died-in-the-field cow," he said, giving the bill a snap. "Here's proof on Wilfred Black. I told you men he wasn't killed. How many times did I tell you men he was alive?"

"Fifty," Arthur said.

"A hundred," I said.

The men let out a big laugh.

"Gotta be at least a million, Ike," the farmhand said.

"But I'll be darned if any of you would listen." Mr. Clarkson held up our handbill to show it to anybody who would look.

Everybody did look, with a good deal of interest.

So far our trick was working. We found out the town men figured that Wilfred Black was dead, and even figured he'd been killed.

Arthur and I stayed close to the men, trying to come up with an idea for getting us out of the mess that would come if Old Man Howe got his hands on the bill.

Mr. Cooper took his turn inspecting the bill. "It looks official. But that doesn't mean it isn't a forgery."

"It's real," Clarkson said.

"I doubt it," Mr. Cooper said. "We'll have to check it against the records at the Land Titles Office in Bosworth."

Half the men agreed with Mr. Clarkson and the other half agreed with Mr. Cooper.

"I agree with Mr. Cooper," Arthur whispered.

"I don't know," I said. "Mr. Clarkson sounds pretty convincing."

We snickered as the argument grew. The Cooper side figured they should hunt down Wilfred Black and teach him a lesson for dragging up all the "old troubles" he caused Mr. Howe. The Clarkson side figured they wouldn't have to because when Mr. Howe read the bill he'd pay good money to any man who'd put Wilfred Black in the ground. At least they were in agreement on Wilfred Black's future.

Arthur and I were standing outside the circle of men as the bill worked its way toward us. Arthur elbowed me and tipped his head toward the outside billboard. "Grab me that Korea bill," he whispered.

I snuck over, pulled it down, and snuck it back to Arthur.

Arthur looked over a short farmer's shoulder, then gave me another head motion. "Get ahead of the bill."

We pushed into the crowd, grumbling about how that rotten Wilfred Black should get a good beating from Mr. Howe. Finally the man on my left got the bill. He looked at it and gave Black a good cussing.

Then I got the bill and started hollering, "Mr. Howe should send that no-good Wilfred Black to Korea!" I waved the bill. "Let the Communists take care of him!"

Everybody went quiet. Even Arthur was staring at me.

Then the man on my left grumbled, "Yeah. Korea. That's where he belongs."

Half the crowd agreed with me and the other half figured Mr. Howe could fix Black better than any Communists. Meanwhile, Arthur switched our bill with the Korea bill, I passed it to the man to my right, and we ducked out of the crowd up Main Street.

"This doesn't end nothing," Arthur said. "Howe will hear about the bill from those men."

"They're just talking," I said, grinning.

Arthur had a poplar leaf stuck under his shirt collar. I went to pull the leaf out when Mr. Howe drove around the corner by the bank, heading toward us. I froze with my hand still in the air like a Nazi salute.

Arthur knocked my arm down and stuffed the bill into his pocket.

I made a quick shoulder check. Sergeant Findley turned onto Main Street from the reserve. Then a man started hollering, "Hey, those kids swiped our bill! This one's for Korea."

Arthur pulled me along the narrow sidewalk that ran beside Clarkson's butcher shop. A second later, Howe's black pickup drove past on Main Street. Ahead of us, the alley was clear all the way to the railway tracks.

Arthur jerked his head toward the reserve. "Happy Valley," he said, and started running.

We ran past Mr. Clarkson's vegetable garden and meat shed, then hopped the short gate and turned toward Gunther's gas station. A car motor roared. Sergeant Findley shot around the corner in front of us, slid sideways, leaned hard toward us, then stopped. Arthur and the car got to the same place at the same time. Arthur slapped his hands on the hood, then turned like nothing happened, and headed back toward Mr. Clarkson's meat shed.

I was right on Arthur's heels.

Ahead of us, the crowd of men was coming along the sidewalk.

Howe pulled up behind us and hollered out his window, "Hold on there, fellas. We don't want no trouble." His voice was old and rough. "We just want to look at that handbill."

I glanced around. We were surrounded. I gave Arthur a nudge. "Give me the bill," I whispered. "All they want is the bill."

He slipped me the map by mistake.

Mr. Howe saw him do it. "I'll take that," he said.

"Oh, that's just some stupid school paper," I said, trying to hide the map as I got the bill from Arthur. "We were just fooling around, that's all."

Mr. Howe grabbed the map. "Well, I'll be a son of a —. It looks like we've caught ourselves a pair'a thieves."

"Ship 'em to Korea!" one of the men hollered.

"Let Mr. Howe at them!" another man called.

Old Man Howe grabbed the bill from my hand. Now he had both papers.

Sergeant Findley jerked open the back door of his car. "Get in!" he shouted.

As Arthur bent over to get into the car, Sergeant Findley kicked him in the rear end. Arthur was trying to get up from where he'd landed on the floorboards when I got tossed on top of him.

"Get off me," Arthur said.

I rolled onto the seat and rubbed my head.

"Jeez," Arthur said, "what's your head made of, rocks?"

"Shush," I whispered, pointing to the driver's window.

Howe and Findley stood with their backs to the door. Howe was talking in a low voice. Every now and then, Sergeant Findley nodded. After a minute, he gave Mr. Howe's arm a friendly slap. "Okay. I'll take care of this."

"Just remember what I told you."

"Don't worry. It won't go any further than you and me."

Sergeant Findley and Howe eased away from the window and headed to Howe's pickup.

"And don't go getting your nose into yesterday's business," Howe added.

"I've got more work than I need in the present."

I was thinking about Howe getting the biggest piece of our land after we lost it to the bank when Arthur started talking really fast.

"You got to get to Mom and tell her where I am."

"In the sergeant's car?"

"Shut up and listen. Get to Catface and find out what this is about, and find Mr. Parks and show him the rest of the deed. Maybe he can help. And find out who Wilfred Black is."

Arthur was talking faster and faster, but he wasn't making a lot of sense. We'd already decided Catface was on his way to Spy Hill jail. Arthur was just saying everything he could think of.

Sergeant Findley pulled open the driver's door and pointed his big finger in Arthur's face. "Shut up!" He got in, slammed the door, and hung his furry arm over the seat. "I don't want to hear as much as a breath outta you little turds." He adjusted the mirror onto my face. "Crescent wrench," he said, and shook his head. I guess he was remembering my lie when he caught me under the Mountie car. "You're smarter than I thought."

In about a minute, I was sitting in the Mountie barracks watching Arthur get dragged up the sidewalk by Sergeant Findley and the constable from the alley.

Arthur was going to jail.

Sergeant Findley glared at me. "If you run, I'll hunt you down."

I stayed put. I was betting that when he was done with Arthur he would throw me in jail, too. I was wrong. He gave me a good bawling out and drove me home. Then I figured he would come in and tell Mom I was a no-good thieving kid. I was wrong there too. He just grabbed a handful of my shirt collar and lifted me off the ground.

I kicked in the air like a snared gopher.

He shook me and hollered at our back door, "Mrs. Samson, this kid of yours was running with thieves!"

Nobody came out. Mom was probably still fighting to get the bobby pins in her hair.

Sergeant Findley gave me one last shake, let me drop, and tramped to his car.

I sat in the dirt and looked up at our back door, then over to Sergeant Findley. He jammed the car into reverse, backed up fast into the lane, and stuck his head out the window.

"You're lucky you're a white Indian or you'd be sitting in jail with your redskin friend."

"Throw me in jail, then. I don't want any favors from you."

"Don't confuse this with any kind'a favor," he said. "If I'm right about your old man, he'll whup you 'til you wish you'd never been born."

He's Ashamed of Himself

Behind me, the outhouse door creaked and Mom stepped out, straightening her dress.

"Where's Arthur?" she asked.

"He's in jail." I felt like crying.

She held me by the shoulders. "Did you and Arthur steal something?"

"No." I had to look at the ground because that was only half true. "We found something that was stolen." I took a breath. "We told Sergeant Findley we just found it, but he didn't believe Arthur."

"Tell me what happened."

I told her the whole story. She said she didn't know anyone by the name of Wilfred Black, but then she didn't move to Grayson until she married Dad. And town folks can be pretty tight-lipped over shameful or dirty deeds.

"Like when we lost our land to the bank," I said. "And Howe got it for next to nothing. And Aunt Molly drowned in the irrigation pond."

"How do you know about those days?"

"I just figured it. You know, from little things a person hears, or when somebody else has had too much to drink. I know a lot." And I told her what I knew.

Mom's face got red when I came to the part about Aunt Molly being too good of a swimmer to drown by mistake, and how she'd fallen into the pond wearing her nightgown, and it had happened in broad daylight. When I got to Aunt Molly getting buried outside the church cemetery, Mom stopped me.

"How drunk was your dad?" she asked.

"Just about fallin' down."

"So you think Emma Howe is living in a shack in the woods?" She shook her head. "I thought she died years ago in the Ponoka sanitarium."

"I know it's her. I saw her. And I saw her that night she jumped from Old Man Howe's truck. Dad can strap me again, but I still say it was her."

"Okay," Mom said, running her fingers through my hair.

"She's got an Indian woman with an ax and a mean dog to make sure she doesn't escape and show the whole town what her dad can turn a person into."

"Craziness comes from some kind of disease. Not from having a father like Mr. Howe."

"Maybe," I said. "But I figure she's a good reason for him to feel ashamed."

"I wouldn't talk about Mr. Howe with such words. There's too many ears in this town listening for that man. And I'd stay away from Emma Howe. We don't need that family's trouble under this roof."

We were quiet for a while. The smell of bread baking came down the stairs. Mom went to see that it wasn't getting burned. She got to the first step and stopped. "You have to take back the rest of the deed. It's not right to steal."

"But they hurt Catface."

I could tell Mom was thinking about how miserable Catface looked, naked and beat up in the back of Howe's truck. When she glanced at the sun, I could see the sadness in her eyes, but she wouldn't let it come out in her words.

"It's not quite noon. There's a good deal of the day left before Dad gets home." She headed into the house. "Don't be late for supper."

I knew what Mom meant. She was giving me permission to hold on to the deed until I had this mystery with Catface figured out. And I had until supper time to get it done. Then the deed would have to go back to Mr. Howe. She also expected me to help Catface and Arthur, too, if I could. Moms are kind of funny about protecting kids. I would help Catface for Mom. I would help Arthur too, and the best way was by figuring out about Catface.

A second later, Mom stuck her head around the doorjamb. "Don't tell Dad what we talked about."

"You mean Aunt Molly?"

Mom nodded.

"Is he ashamed of his own sister?"

"He's ashamed of himself," Mom said, and turned back to her baking.

You Have a Dilemma, That's for Sure

I ducked under a piece of eavestrough hanging from the roof, followed the wheel ruts to the end of our lane, and headed up the road to Mr. Parks's house. I was thinking about Aunt Molly. She was my dad's oldest sister. She died in 1933, six months after the bank took our land. I never knew her, being as I wasn't born for another seven years.

Sometimes Dad gets melancholy. He manages by drinking. During some of those times, he'll talk to Mom about Aunt Molly. His sister got awfully bleak when we lost our land to Mr. Howe. The town people started whispering about how poor the Samsons were and how Molly would be lucky to find an Indian to marry her. Shortly after that, she went to bed and didn't get out until she decided to drown herself in the irrigation pond.

I followed the road to a fallen poplar. There, I crossed the ditch and walked along the bank, keeping the cattails and tall grass between me and the gravel road. I used this route when I wanted to sneak to town. It wasn't the fastest way to Mr. Parks's house, but it was the safest. Mr. Howe and Sergeant Findley would be easy to spot from the ditch, and hiding was easier in tall grass than on a one-car gravel road.

I worked my way up the ditch until I reached the irrigation pond. The high water had pushed out the ditch banks a little farther every year until it made a pond about a hundred yards long and fifty yards wide.

On the far bank, a yearling whitetail deer watched me.

Keeping an eye on the road leading to Howe's farm, I slipped in behind a clump of willows and sat on the bank.

The pond was the deep green of summer wheat. A gentle current flowed from the ditch, making the grass seem as if it was swimming. My own shadow drifted just below the surface. And the air was full of Aunt Molly's shame.

From the direction of Howe's farm came the steady *pop pop* of a grain auger engine. Behind it, a three-ton truck rumbled up the road. Albert Loewan was driving and two Indian men sat, holding scoop shovels, on a big pile of grain in the back.

One of the men was Arthur's dad. He stared through the thicket of willows and looked right at me.

I quickly turned away.

The deer slipped into the bushes.

I could feel that gaze on the back of my head, like Arthur's dad was looking at my thoughts and wondering where Arthur was.

I fought my way through the willows and came out onto the fairgrounds. A hundred yards in front of me was the trapshooting range.

I ran through the pieces of clay pigeons and shotgun shells, past the squat lean-to where the launcher sat with its bent arm, and headed to the alley behind Mr. Parks's house.

Maybe he wouldn't even be home. I hadn't given that much thought until now.

I knocked on the back door and waited.

Nothing.

I knocked again.

I was about to go when the door opened.

Mr. Parks stood with a silly grin on his face. He had on blue jeans and cowboy boots and a T-shirt that said "The Calgary Stampede 1952" on the front. He held out his arms and slowly turned. On the back of the T-shirt was a picture of the Three Stooges.

"What do you think?" he asked. "Pretty nice, huh?" He made a "nyuck nyuck" sound. When I didn't do anything but stare, he got serious. "I thought you liked the Three Stooges."

"I do. Kind'a."

"Kind'a? Are you okay, Will? And please don't tell me you're in trouble."

"Arthur's in jail."

Mr. Parks looked down the alley toward the Mountie barracks, then said in a quiet voice, "Come in before they see you."

I told Mr. Parks everything.

"Of course, your mom is right," he finally said. "But I'm not so sure that she was actually giving you permission. On the other hand, I agree that you don't need to return the deed just yet. It would be interesting to see what the Land Titles Office has to say about it first."

He went to his refrigerator and got a bottle of Coke. Curly's stomach got really wide when Mr. Parks bent over. He put the Coke on the table and pushed it over to me. "I get them from Gunther's gas station. Be careful. They can freeze your eyes right out of their sockets." He made a bug-eyed stare as if his eyes were frozen.

I drank the Coke.

Mr. Parks wandered around the room. First he looked out the window and rubbed his chin. Then he wiped a rag across the top edge of the sink and rubbed his chin again. When I finished the Coke and had a good burp and got my eyesight back, Mr. Parks was leaning back in his chair, looking across the table at me.

"You have a dilemma, that's for sure. You could make a deal with Mr. Howe. You could give him the deed in exchange for Arthur. That would work, I believe." He gave his chin one more rub. It was a pretty good-sized chin. "But I also believe, from what you've told me, that Arthur would rather stay in jail than give in to Mr. Howe or Sergeant Findley. Arthur has a strong will. But a strong will can get a man in a good deal of trouble — even more than it can get him out of."

"But what if it's against the law to give the deed back to Mr. Howe? What if Mr. Howe's the thief? What if he's stealing from Wilfred Black?" I asked.

"Mr. X."

I nodded.

"Good point. It seems you have many dilemmas." He got up and wandered around the room again. "First we need to find out who Wilfred Black is. You'll have as good a chance as anybody of finding that out. Go to the library and do some research." He gave me a teacher's grin, like he was saying, "See how important school is?" Then he said, "Are you still on good terms with Jane Howe?"

"She helped me do research for all that writing you made me do last year."

"She's a good librarian and a fine person."

"Do you think she'll tell me about her dad's dirty business?"

"She may know less than you do, Will."

"What am I looking for with all this research?" I asked, giving him my best confused-student look.

"I don't know. Wilfred Black. Emma Howe. Mr. Howe. Connections. Some kind of connection."

"And Catface?"

"Of course. But Catface comes in at the end. Wilfred Black is at the beginning. Start there. We know more about the beginning. And maybe the beginning will be recorded somewhere."

"Like in the library."

Mr. Parks nodded. He took my empty bottle and gave the table a wipe where I'd smeared some Coke.

I headed up the alley and thought about Arthur. I was really close to the jail. I wanted to sneak over and crawl along that concrete ledge and look through the window and give Arthur a wave and say I would help him get out even if I had to run a tractor through the wall.

Then I got a bad feeling. Maybe he was all beat up and lying on that cold floor. I turned down the street and headed for the library.

I didn't want to see Arthur beat up.

Closer Than We Seemed

I took a shortcut down the alley behind Frankie's store, through Cooper's machinery yard and out toward Main Street. I crossed in front of Pots's insurance and stepped out into the street just as the three-ton truck came whining down the east ramp of the Wheat Pool elevator. When the truck rounded the corner from behind Gunther's gas station, Arthur's dad was standing in the box looking down the street at me.

I wanted to run. Then I wanted to holler over my shoulder to Arthur, like he was with me. But I just stood there like a dummy, staring at Arthur's dad.

The truck made a quick swerve toward me.

I jumped for the sidewalk, plowed into Pots's door, and landed on my back in front of his desk.

He glared over his half glasses.

Albert Loewan laughed out the truck window. "Get off the road, you stupid kid!"

Pots made a sweeping motion with his hand, like he was getting rid of dirt. "Same goes for my office."

I got up and grumbled under my breath.

"Whud you say?"

"I said, I'm going."

"Darn right you are," he said, and made a quick I'll-get-you move.

I beat him to the door and slammed it closed behind me.

Down Main Street, Arthur's dad was still holding on to the big wooden tailgate, watching me, swaying with the truck as it headed back toward Howe's farm. He was worried.

Arthur and I were always together. His mom used to tease us. "We'll have to put you two in the ground together." Then she would laugh and say, "Even if only one of you is dead."

Arthur had said I should go tell his mom that he'd got thrown in jail, but I figured no one else would tell her for a few hours, at least. Indians never get much news from town. I even heard of an Indian fellow who got killed in the war, and the government didn't even bother to tell his mom. She heard about it after the war was over and the other Indian soldiers came home. They say she was standing right on Main Street when the bus pulled up. All the soldiers piled out and got hugged and kissed by moms, sisters, wives, kids, dads and everybody.

That was how she found out — her son didn't get off the bus.

I headed to the library. Inside, Jane Howe was sorting a pile of books at her desk. She didn't look like her crazy sister. Her sister looked more like Mr. Howe's sister than Jane's. I guess being crazy can make a person old.

I decided to get my research done first, so if I had to ask Jane Howe some rough questions, I'd have a way of telling if she was with me or her dad.

I thought about the deed and that it had been signed on March 9, 1917. During the First World War — just one month before the battle of Vimy Ridge. It felt like I was back in Mr. Parks's class the day he said we had to write an essay about the greatest victory the Canadian army had in World War I. I worked on the essay for a whole week. Now Vimy Ridge is burned into my brain like I was there.

I went to the aisles I knew well and slid out *The History of Grayson: 1900 to 1945*. I sat on the floor between the shelves and opened the book to the long list of names of men who died in World War I. Near the top of the first row, just below the name John Anderson was Wilfred Black, and beside his name was a little star. At the bottom of the page was another star. It said, "Died on Vimy Ridge, April 9, 1917."

I checked every page, and then I checked again. There were no pictures of Wilfred Black.

I looked through the rows of books and on to where Jane Howe was comparing library cards to book titles. I wondered how much she knew about her sister, if she thought Emma died years ago in the Ponoka asylum, like my mom did. I wondered if Emma Howe had been made crazy by Wilfred Black getting killed in the trenches. Maybe she didn't even know he was dead, and that's why she called Arthur "Willy." Jane had to be twenty years younger than Emma, I'd guess. She wouldn't have been born until after Wilfred Black died. I wondered if she even knew who he was.

I walked over to her desk, tapping the book on my leg.

Her face was red and a bit damp from the heat. I set the book on her pile.

She ran her fingers over the cover. "I like this one," she said. "Local history is important to remember. I believe it is possible to learn from the past." She carefully lined up the edges of the book with the others in the pile.

I could feel the sweat beading on my forehead as I tried to word my question.

"Sure is hot," she said.

"Yeah, I guess." I wiped my shirt sleeve across my face. "I was wondering about a man named Wilfred Black. He's in the book but there's no picture or anything said about him."

"Now isn't that curious," she said. "You're the second person in as many days to ask that very question."

"Was it Arthur?" I asked before thinking.

"No, a tall skinny Blackfoot boy."

I described Catface.

"That's the one," she said, sounding very pleased. "He seemed nervous. Rather like you do right now. And when Sergeant Findley drove past, he disappeared up Main Street before I could show him this book."

I glanced out the window and back at Jane Howe.

"You don't know Wilfred Black?"

"No. Why?"

"Your dad knows him." I tried not to sound like I was accusing her of something, but it didn't work.

"My father is an old man. He knows many people of whom I have never even heard."

"You don't know him from rumors? In this town?"

"Why are you talking to me like this, Will? Am I suddenly no longer your friend?"

"Wilfred Black's name is on a deed to a piece of your dad's farm."

"What?"

We both glanced out the window as a truck drove past.

I told her everything Arthur and I had seen when her dad and his men were chasing Catface in the night. I stopped short of telling her about her sister.

"I think your dad did something bad to Wilfred Black."

"How could you even suggest such a thing, Will? Besides, it was so long ago. The best you could do is assume."

She got up and slowly walked over to the door. It looked like she was going to ask me to get out of the library and never come back until I could talk more civil.

I stopped behind her and looked out the glass to Main Street. I couldn't get the sound of Emma Howe out of my head, how she had begged the pockfaced woman, how she had cried like a little girl when the woman said it wasn't her Willy and that she was an old fool.

"I heard your sister begging Alice to let her Willy come home. Then I heard her crying like a little girl. Wilfred Black is her Willy. Isn't he?"

Now Jane Howe's reflection stood beside my own in the big window, together, looking out over the town, closer than we seemed.

"You know about Emma being alive?" I asked.

"Yes," she said. "But not until just recently. I have yet to see her. Frankly, I can't remember if we ever spoke."

I stepped past her and reached for the door.

"Please don't judge me when you don't know any of the details," she said, then took a long breath and let it out slowly. "Everyone has some shameful thing in their lives. The Howes are no exception. *I* am no exception."

"I don't have one."

"If that's really true, it's only because you're not very old. Give yourself some time."

"Your dad is trying to get that deed back. And I think he did something bad to Emma."

Jane's body stiffened as I watched her in the window glass. In a second, she seemed angry. "My father put Emma away because it was necessary. If that bothers you, then maybe you should talk to him."

"Okay," I said, trying not to look at her reflection. "I thought you'd help me. I didn't think you'd be on the other side."

I could feel her hand reaching for my shoulder, but I wouldn't let her touch me. Before I could push open the door and step out onto the street, she reached past me and turned the lock.

A Hateful Man

We sat on the floor between the bookshelves closest to the door. I pulled up my knees and stared at her.

Jane pulled up hers, too, and stared back.

She looked like my mom getting ready to tell me something that made her heart ache.

"I haven't spoken to my father in years."

"I don't like him either."

"That's not the reason, Will. It's just that we look at the world differently. We disagree on things ... about this town."

"He doesn't like Indians."

"That's true, but he's not alone."

She went on to say that her father could be a hateful man, that he had become worse with age, and that he'd thrown her out of his house. She said she had never known her sister. And for most of her life she'd believed her father when he told her Emma was dead.

"She's not," I said.

"Yes," she said. "Arthur's grandfather told me. But I'm ashamed to say I haven't been ... brave enough to go see her." She leaned forward. "You said you talked to Emma. How is she? Are they treating her well?"

"You mean Alice?"

"I don't know any of her nurses."

"Alice isn't a nurse," I said. "She's a guard."

"I guess that's probably true," she said. "The Ponoka asylum isn't a place I know much about."

"Ponoka? She's not in Ponoka. She lives on that piece of land that belongs to Wilfred Black."

"My father's land? You mean she's here? In Grayson? What are you saying?"

"I thought you said Arthur's grandpa told you."

"Yes, of course he did." She looked confused. "No, he didn't say exactly where she was. I just assumed —"

"Maybe you should talk to your father," I said.

Her face went red and her eyes got a little wet. Before she could cry, a black Fargo truck pulled up against the sidewalk and Old Man Howe stepped out onto the street. A second later, he was standing in front of the glass door, jerking on the handle and hollering.

"Open this damned door!"

Jane jumped to her feet and took my hand, and we ran between the bookshelves to the back of the building. She fought with the barrel bolt holding the door closed, then hit the handle with a heavy book.

When she flung the door open, Howe was standing, waiting. He grabbed my hair and jerked me into Jane's leg.

She swung the book hard. It hit his hand with a loud crack. The sound echoed in my head as I ran down the alley and up the side street toward the railway station. When I heard Howe cussing his daughter, I slowed to a walk, giving him a chance to catch up to me.

An Old Fool

I stopped on the platform and stared out onto the reserve. The air was hot and still and smelled of melted tar. I didn't run when Howe's truck turned the corner by the post office and headed toward me. I was thinking about Big Lodge Pole's words Arthur had whispered to himself when we were lying in the prairie grass making wishes on the stars: "Make my enemy brave and strong, so that if defeated, I will not be ashamed."

Howe stopped and got out of his truck. His face was puffy and red. When I didn't run, he hit me with the back of his hand. And when I got up and he knocked me down again, I knew I wasn't going to run anymore. He turned away like he had just thought maybe Jane would be running, but she was staring down the road ahead of her as if her dad and I didn't even exist.

"Your old man needs to beat some sense into that redskin brain of yours," he said.

"My dad could whup you in a second," I said. I wanted to rub my face where he'd hit me.

This time Howe swung a tight bony fist. But I turned my jaw and he nearly fell over when he spun around. He caught his balance and swung again. This time he stumbled and fell.

"I'll show you what for." He cussed me. "I've got ways to whip a man you've never dreamed of."

"You're just an old fool," I said, and headed down the platform.

The truck door opened and slammed closed. "Don't look at me!" his muffled voice shouted at Jane. "What kind of daughter shames her own father? Dammit, I said look the other way!"

I headed down the tracks toward Arthur's house.

Still Young

I sat on the steps, leaned my back against the door, and stared at the mess in the yard. The blankets that Arthur's family used for sleeping were strewn all over. The woodpile was pulled down until not one piece of wood was stacked on another.

A large poplar log lay facing me on the outhouse path, its empty crack where Arthur and I had hid the deed drooped like a sad mouth.

A mumbling sound came from the outhouse. A second later, the door squeaked open and Arthur's grandpa stepped out and headed down the path toward me. His chest was bare. The two jagged scars from a long-ago sun dance, where the sticks had torn through his flesh, seemed slightly pink, as if that part of him was still young.

He sat beside me and put his tin cup of tea on the ground between us. On top of that, he set his big piece of bannock.

"Arthur's in jail," I said to the ground between my feet.

Arthur's grandpa took a bit of bannock and spit it out. He took a drink of tea and spit it out, too. "Tastes like poop," he said and got up. "You want some fresh stuff?"

"Sure."

He pushed by me to get inside the house. A few minutes later, he returned with two cups of tea and two pieces of bannock piled high with strawberry jam. We sat together and ate.

"Better," he said after a few bites.

My mouth was full, so I just nodded.

He drank the last of his tea, poured the leaves on the ground, and tapped the cup against a piece of firewood.

I washed the bannock down with a mouthful of tea. "What happened?" I asked. "Was Sergeant Findley here? Is he the one who did this? Did he tell you Arthur's in jail? Did he find the —"

"White men talk too much," Arthur's grandpa said, and looked at my empty cup. "You want more?"

"Okay."

This time the tea had extra sugar in it, and it was strong, too. The numbness of the day settled from me like somebody had suddenly stopped stirring a pail of dirty water. I even gave some thought to talking again, but didn't. I was always getting into trouble with Indians for talking when I should be listening.

Arthur's grandpa sat without moving, his thick forearms resting on his knees, his hands hanging easy in the air. Many years ago, he'd been a warrior. He rode with Lame Bull in Montana, he was there when Red Crow killed his own brother, and he was at Blackfoot Crossing when Crowfoot signed Treaty Number 7. His smell reminded me of Arthur. And it was hard for me not to think how Arthur'd said these chiefs were as great as any president or prime minister or king or queen. It was hard to sit beside somebody who was more of a man than any white man I'd ever known.

When I turned to him, he was watching me.

"You feel better?" he asked.

"Yeah. I mean, I was hungry. I guess I forgot to stop to eat. Maybe all that running around used up my energy —" I closed my mouth when I realized I was doing it again.

"Good," he said, and stood. "Stack the wood and shake out the blankets."

The blankets were quite a mess, with grass and dirt stuck all over them. Arthur's mom would be awfully mad. I shook them out, then put them back in their place in the house. As I set the table upright and re-stood the chairs, I figured it was a good thing Arthur's mom was someplace else. She'd have murder in her eyes if she saw what Sergeant Findley had done to her new table and chairs.

When I finished the woodpile, Arthur's grandpa said, "Come with me."

He walked down a packed-dirt trail, past the Indian hospital, and out into the prairie southeast of

Heavy Shield School. When we finally stopped, the sun was setting and the air had gone cool.

"Arthur's teaching you to be an Indian?"

"I'm learning pretty good," I said. "For a white kid. If I was Cree, I could learn a bit quicker, seeing that the Cree are already Indians of some kind."

When I finally finished, Arthur's grandpa said, "Give me your clothes."

"What?"

He pointed to my shirt and pants.

I took them off and handed them to him.

He pointed to my underwear and my shoes.

I turned away and took them off, too.

Then he pointed to a tall hill. Its sides were steep and covered with short grass and cacti. A shallow valley seemed to go all around its base like a dry moat.

"Come back when you learn what it means to be an Indian," he said.

"Will you teach me?" I asked.

Before I could say anything else, Arthur's grandpa touched his ears, then his mouth. "Listen two times. Talk one."

I climbed to the top of the hill and watched him disappear over the horizon. There was nothing on the hill, no food, no water, no fire. I was all alone and cold.

It was dark when I went down into the valley where the grass was taller and the air was warmer, but something was following me, an animal with yellow eyes and whose breathing sounded like a low growl. It forced me up the hill. By midnight I was curled up, trying to get warmth from my own body, and whimpering, because I thought the torment would never end. When the Big Dipper was sitting flat above the northern horizon, I ran screaming down the hill, but the animal caught me before I hit the valley floor. It knocked me down and snarled and snapped its teeth in my face. Again, he forced me up the hill. The dawn was still forever away. The animal began circling the hill, pacing the valley, waiting for me to run again. I pulled a piece of cactus from my ankle, hurled it at the animal, hollered at it to come and get me, if it dared. "I'll kill you with my bare hands. And if you kill me, I don't care." It didn't come. Then I cussed Arthur's grandpa. When the false dawn arrived, I was crying like a baby. As the last stars disappeared ahead of the sun, I fell asleep.

I dreamed Arthur and I were in the medicine lodge at the sun dance, where boys became men who then became warriors. Arthur's grandpa cut Arthur's breast four times. As he pushed the sharpened sticks through one hole and out the other, Arthur's body trembled, but Arthur didn't cry. A second man made the same cuts on Arthur's back, pushed two more sticks through, and hung an Indian drum from them for extra weight to help Arthur tear the wood from his flesh. Arthur's grandpa struck the sticks in Arthur's chest twice so hard that Arthur fell back. I didn't think he'd be able to stand, but he did, without any help. All around me the men called out in Blackfoot, loud words that I could not understand. And when Arthur's grandpa lashed the sticks with leather hanging from the medicine pole, Arthur called out my name — not Will, but the name I'd earned from my great deeds as a white man becoming an Indian: He Runs Down the Hill Screaming.

Are You Ashamed?

When I woke, the sun was high and hot. My clothes sat folded in a pile. On them was a piece of stiff cloth rolled like a tube and tied with a strip of leather. Beside them, a large wolflike dog lay with her chin on the ground between her front paws.

I rolled quickly onto my side and kicked at her. She jumped and ran round me, bouncing up and down and snapping her teeth. When she passed my clothes, she bit the cloth tube and shook it, then dropped it near my hand, stepped back, and tipped her head sideways.

"Oh brother," I said. "If it was you in the valley last night, you were a lot tougher in the dark."

She wagged her tail and glanced at the cloth.

I lay there for a long time, with the dog trying to get me to throw her toy. I felt miserable that I'd left Arthur in jail and not even tried to tell his mom where he was. I felt more miserable that I'd let Sergeant Findley find the deed. And I felt worst about failing Arthur's grandpa's Indian test. I could hardly look the dog in the eye. My Aunt Molly had been so ashamed of our family losing our land that she'd drowned herself. I'd felt ashamed of myself when Arthur said I was no better than an Indian. Now I wasn't even good enough to be an Indian.

I stared up at the sky and the fluffy white clouds. I drifted in and out of sleep. Beneath me, the earth was warm and quiet, like a still pond. Something touched my arm. Then a strange voice spoke. "Are you ashamed of me?" it asked. When I opened my eyes, the blue sky had become water, and Aunt Molly was floating facedown above me, her white nightgown drifting around her body, like a cloud in a windless sky.

I woke with a jerk when the dog dropped her toy on my chest.

She had worked the leather tie so much that it had unknotted and the cloth unrolled. Inside was the deed to Wilfred Black's farm. She moved her eyebrows from side to side, between me and the paper.

All the pages were there except for the last one and the map. I rolled them back into the cloth, got dressed, and stuffed the roll under my shirt. When I looked back, just for a second I saw age in the dog's eyes even though she was still young. It was the same look I'd seen in Arthur's grandpa. It made me feel good.

I thought maybe I hadn't failed the old man's test, after all. Maybe it was still going on. Whatever happened next, I'd trust my instincts. Maybe I'd even listen twice and not talk at all.

I Called Her Leader

I headed down the hill toward Arthur's house. Once we got to the small valley at the bottom of the hill, the dog turned me in the direction of Emma Howe's woods. When I ignored her, she growled low and harsh. I still didn't listen. In the next breath, she began circling me, her fur standing rough over her body, her eyes as yellow as moonlight.

"Okay. Jeez," I said, and started for the woods.

She ran ahead, jumping at small ground birds and sniffing gopher holes.

We came at Emma Howe's woods from the south, the opposite direction Arthur and I had used the day before. The light wind blew on my face, keeping our scent away from the shack. I'd worked up my fear of the pockfaced woman and her wild dog to where I was sweating and my breathing was short and quick. I'd've swallowed, but I couldn't make any spit.

The dog's shoulder touched my leg. Her body felt hot as she glared into the trees.

"Can you smell trouble?" I whispered.

Her eyebrows shifted in my direction, then along the trees' edge.

"Okay. I'm ready."

We moved slowly in the tall grass, stopping every dozen paces, feeling our way into the tightly spaced poplars, then turning back before we got so stuck we'd never escape. We made it past the poplars, but that just led us into a wall of scrub willow with branches like spears.

The old trees towered above us, but they might as well have been a hundred miles away. Woods like this didn't just grow on the prairie — somebody had planted them to keep somebody from wandering in, or to keep somebody from wandering out.

I followed the dog. When mosquitoes rose from the grass and gathered around my head, I was ready to give up and go home. But she stopped at a dark outline that looked like a tunnel big enough for a car. I decided to give her an Indian name. I called her She Leads the Way, but shortened it to Leader for convenience.

We smelled the smoke before we saw it. A half hour later, we saw its thin white cloud drifting among the treetops. Then we saw the outline of the shack.

As I listened for the black dog, I touched Leader's shoulder. Her fur was hotter still. I didn't like to think about her and that mean dog. He was a good deal bigger. I just hoped she was faster, because I didn't think she was tougher.

A sharp *whack* echoed through the woods as an ax hit.

The sound made my skin jump.

Leader froze for a long second, then sunk into the grass as she crept forward.

In another minute, we were close enough to see the back of the woman's head, her short oily black hair and the ridges of muscle across her shoulders. She turned slowly, as if she had caught our scent. The chopping had turned her skin a deep red, with white lumps where the pocks had been.

She scanned the woods, then set a log, took a two-handed stroke, drove the ax clean through the log, and buried the blade deep in the chopping stump. When she jerked the ax, the stump came off the ground like a piece of kindling.

Then I heard it — the sniffing, gurgling sound of a dog tracking something in the woods. I turned as a thick rope twisted through the grass like a snake. My eyes slid along its length, but before I could see him, the black shadow shot through the air, hitting heavy, with all four feet flat on my chest.

I gasped and landed on my back. The dog stood on my body and looked down at me. A line of drool hung from his jowls.

"Kill, dog!" Pockface called.

In a second, he was ripping at me. I pulled my arms free and grabbed for the rope, but missed, catching a handful of damp fur instead. He thrashed his head and beat at me with his claws. I got hold of his ear with my free hand and jammed my thumb deep into the opening.

He grunted, twisted loose, and bit for my head.

I turned and saw a tan-colored blur, hard and silent like an arrow, flash through the grass. Leader hit the black dog from the side and knocked him over, tumbling with him and disappearing into the tall grass in a fury of snarls and snapping teeth.

Then it was silent.

I pushed myself through the dead leaves and sat against a tree. My shirt was torn, I had scratches on my neck and chest and both arms, and one bite went clear through the center of my left hand.

In another second, both dogs were standing.

The black dog was sniffing Leader, and Leader was sniffing him.

"Kill!" Pockface hollered again.

But Leader was headed for the wheat field. The black dog had his tail straight in the air and was doing his best to keep up. Behind them, Pockface was cussing in Blackfoot as she ran after them, the heavy steel ax in her hand.

By a Promise of Land

The door was held shut with an oversized barrel bolt wired down so it couldn't be wiggled loose by somebody determined to get out.

Inside, it was quiet.

I leaned against the jamb. If the fear in my blood hadn't worn off and got the bites hurting so bad that I couldn't lift my arms, I would've knocked. Instead, I put all I had left into untwisting the wire and wiggling the bolt loose. My legs melted away, and I slid down the door into the dirt.

The door opened with the weight of my shoulders, and I tumbled into the room.

The linoleum felt cool through the rips in my shirt. The air smelled old and damp, like the inside of a trunk stuffed with memories.

I didn't see her standing in the dim light until it was too late. She lunged at me with a broomstick sharpened to a thin spear, hooked her foot in her nightdress, and stumbled toward me, the stick swinging wildly as she fell. I kicked in the air, missed her, and deflected the stick. I thought it was going to miss me. But as the stick fell flat with my body, the thin spear point caught my shirt, and she landed on the blunt end. My breath left my body in a long moan as her weight pushed the stick under the flesh of my breast. In a second, she was lying on top of me, her eyes wild and confused.

Then she was running, her dirty nightdress billowing out behind her.

I lay for a long while watching the stick rise and fall with my breathing. It felt like nothing at all — no bleeding, no pain, not even any fear, just a tingling all over, as if my whole body had fallen asleep and was just starting to wake. I ran my fingers down the shaft to where it pierced my breast, then along the six inches it traveled under my skin. I knew I wasn't going to die, but I didn't know much else.

Then the tingling passed. Behind it, the pain grew inside me like a wildfire rolling across the prairie.

I grasped the shaft with two hands, bit down on my teeth, and pulled. It didn't budge. In a second, I was throwing up on the floor. Then everything went black.

In the next breath, I was back on the hill where Arthur's grandpa had left me the night before. All around me was the sun dance. I was standing now with Arthur as he leaned away from the medicine pole and jerked his body against the wood and leather and pain that bound him to childhood. The sound of

Arthur's singing raged in my head like a thousand years of boys becoming men.

When I opened my eyes, Emma Howe was standing over me. I didn't move as she lowered the knife and ran it along the mound of skin. She put her hand over my mouth, muffling my screams, as she lifted the stick from my body, and threw it into the corner.

Sitting on the edge of the mattress of the old iron-framed bed were the pages of the deed.

"Who are you?" she whispered. "How did you get the deed to this land? Where is my husband?"

I looked away from where she knelt at my side.

"Answer me," she said.

"Help me up."

"You'll stay where I can watch you."

"I just want to sit, is all."

Her hands felt warm as she slid one behind my back and the other under my legs, but instead of pushing me to the wall, she stood, holding me like a child. When she set me on her bed and piled pillows behind my back, I knew she wasn't going to hurt me again.

She pulled a wooden apple box full of pickle jars from under the table and began reading labels.

I glanced around the room, which was all the shack was, just one room with a woodstove, a table and a bed with iron legs. And pictures. Lots of pictures sitting on a ledge halfway up the wall and all the way around the room, the table, the windowsill, and even on the floor. From where I was lying, I'd guess there were only three to four different pictures.

That was it.

I looked down at the ones I'd knocked over when I fell. In one, a man and a woman were standing with their arms around each other. In another was the same man and woman, but the woman was holding a baby. In the last one, the man stood, alone, dressed in a uniform from the First World War.

I turned back to Emma. She was standing with a jar in one hand and an old bedsheet in the other. She didn't seem crazy so much as lost. She was the young woman in the picture. I could see that. I figured the man was Wilfred Black. And the baby, well, I didn't have to do much figuring there.

Those pictures told me why Old Man Howe wanted to keep it a secret, and why Jane Howe had believed her sister had died in the Ponoka asylum. I guess part of it was because Emma was not much more than a girl, about sixteen, and she had a baby. That was bad enough. But Wilfred Black was an Indian. A tall, handsome Blackfoot Indian.

"Where is my husband?" she asked again.

I ran my fingers across my chest. The skin was jagged and damp with blood.

"He died at Vimy Ridge. April 9, 1917. I'm sorry nobody told you."

She sat on the bed with the jar and sheet resting in her lap. "My dad promised Wilfred he could have this land if he went to war. He even gave this deed to Wilfred. But when Wilfred left, Dad took my baby. What happened to my baby? His name is Samuel."

I had heard of Samuel Black. Actually, I had read about him in the Grayson history book. He'd worked his whole life as Old Man Howe's hired hand. That is, until he ended up on one of the lists of men who died in war. An artillery shell blew up his landing craft at Dieppe.

That was a different war.

"I don't know," I lied.

That was when I heard a truck engine rumble to a stop and the sound of men talking. In a second a dog was grunting and rooting at the crack under the door. I went to get up, but Emma put her hand on my good shoulder.

A dog ran around the house and growled, but it wasn't the black dog or Leader.

"Alice!" Albert Loewan hollered.

Emma glanced at me, then at the door.

"It's your dad's foreman," I said. "He's come to do your dad's dirty work."

The dog was digging at the sill as I swung my legs to the floor and stood.

"He has come for you. Hasn't he?" she asked.

"No, not for me, not exactly."

"The deed?"

"He'll hide it for another thirty-five years. Or 'til every person related to Wilfred Black is dead."

She looked at me amazed. "It was all a lie, wasn't it?" She turned to the door. "He sent Willy to die in that war, for nothing. For a lie."

Then came voices from outside. "Fred!" Loewan shouted. "Check down the tracks. See if Alice is over there. I'll check the shack."

I crossed the room to the window and pushed on the heavy shutter with my elbow. "Can you open it for me? Can you help me get away?"

Emma touched my arm. "Samuel," she whispered. "Where is he? What has he done to my baby?"

I didn't answer. Her father had sent Wilfred Black and her son to war. He didn't kill them, not directly, just sent them to die. By a promise of land. By a signed deed.

"Alice!" Loewan called. "Where are you? You sleeping some place, wasting Mr. Howe's money? You lazy, no-good redskin."

Emma took my arm and pulled me toward the door. "No. Don't give me up," I whispered. "They'll beat me."

She looked sorrowfully at me, like maybe she was seeing her own child. "I'm not giving you up," she said, glancing back at the window. "Even if I could open those shutters, the dogs would be on you before you got to the trees. Believe me, I've tried."

She pushed me into a corner, tight to the wall. Then she put her hand, with the deed in it, behind her back, messed up her hair, and opened the door over me.

The dog growled. Through the crack, I could see it jump for the opening. Emma raised her knee and caught the dog in the chest. It let out a yelp.

"There's no dogs allowed in this house."

"Hold on, Miss Howe," Albert Loewan said. "Me and Fred won't hurt you. We're just following your dad's orders. All we want is that Samson boy."

"A little one with shifty eyes?"

"That's the one. He thieved from your dad. Right outta his own house."

"Alice chased him down the tracks, that way." She pointed. "And if I didn't have to stay in this cabin, I'd be after him myself."

"Well, that son of a —" Loewan cussed, then hollered, "Fred, they're down the tracks. Come on, Sniffer."

Sniffer and Loewan headed for the tracks.

Emma closed the door, rolled the deed in the cloth, and stuffed it under my shirt. "This doesn't belong to me. You'll have to find Samuel or ... his heir. But first we'll mend your wounds, then maybe you'll get out of here alive."

She went back to the bed and returned with the jar. In it was something green and stinky, smelling of rotten leaves. She smeared big lumps of the goo on my dog bites and the cut on my chest, then wrapped both with strips torn from the sheet. She pushed the door open and glanced in the direction the men had gone. "Okay," she said. "I know where there's a secret trail."

I was turning green from the smell.

She led me through the woods to a spot where the willows had been planted so close together that they'd grown into a thick wall of twisted branches. Maybe a skinny squirrel couldn't even get through. She moved the grass and the deadfall and uncovered a narrow hole. It was a tunnel through the willows and out into the fields.

I stared at it for a long second before I said, "I have to know something."

"All right. But you don't have much time."

"Are you ashamed because you had an Indian baby?"

She almost laughed. "I'd be a soulless woman to be ashamed of my own child."

"Why are you a prisoner in this place?"

"My father *is* a soulless man who hates everything he cannot control."

"I have an Indian friend," I said, but didn't know why.

Her eyes got all cloudy. "They're coming for you."

Behind us, the men and Sniffer had turned back. I guess they'd figured out Emma's trick. Then I heard the black dog barking and the pockfaced woman cussing.

"If you run hard, you'll reach Buffalo Creek in twenty minutes." She spoke like she had made the run before. "Get into the water and stay close to the edge. Turn upstream toward the reserve. Go at least fifty yards before you run into the field. Leave plenty of footprints, then get back into the water and swim or float downstream."

She was talking pretty fast. I just hoped I could remember it all.

"The dogs will lose your scent in the water," she said, "if you're lucky."

I looked at my arms and then back at the tunnel.

"Don't worry. They'll feel better soon. And the water won't hurt the poultice. It's a Blackfoot cure."

I bent over and started into the hole.

Emma gave me a friendly push on the rear end to get me going.

She was right. My arms worked pretty good and my chest felt good, too, but they were bleeding again — a kind of water and blood mix. I was leaving a good trail for the dogs. But the pressure was gone, and I felt full of energy.

I wiggled from side to side and pushed with my feet. But as I worked through the tunnel, the dogs' barking grew louder and louder.

I'll Skin Him Alive

I broke from the tunnel, ran into a heavy growth of thistles and stinkweed, fell, and jammed my body between two young poplars. I rolled the smallest tree flat with my shoulder and tore out over the wheat field to the east bank of Buffalo Creek.

There I bent over, cupping my hands on my knees. My arms and legs were green and wet from slicing through the tall grain.

My spit tasted like old pennies and my chest burned.

I took a couple of deep breaths. In front of me, a path lay like somebody had drawn a line through the grain. At the woods' edge, four dark spots appeared, moving quickly this way and that.

I'd bet the dogs were running in circles, barking, and sniffing for my scent. Albert Loewan was hollering orders. Fred was waving and calling the dogs, because he'd just seen me — the lone dark spot standing by the creek as a green wave passed over the wheat, swallowing the path.

I turned to the creek. There I slid down the bank, put the deed in my mouth, and headed upstream like Emma had said. I only went twenty yards before I ran into the field. I made a tight circle, then dashed back to the creek, and slipped into the water.

I floated for as long as my nerves could stand, then crawled up the far bank and ran toward Mrs. Bowman's farm. It probably took twenty minutes to cover the three miles, but it felt like forever. When I climbed over the tailgate of one of Mrs. Bowman's loaded grain trucks, the dogs were loping past the boxcar at the east end of her property. As the truck pulled away from the grain bin, Albert Loewan's old pickup turned down the dirt trail toward it.

"Hey, Jim Samson!" Loewan called out his window. "Where's that kid of yours?"

"Ain't seen him since early yesterday," my dad said.

"You see him, tell him I'm looking for him."

"You and half the town."

"How about you, Tom?" Loewan asked. "You see him run by here?"

"Haven't seen nothing but wheat in two days," the driver said.

I lay on the bed of wheat, breathing deep and hard, as the truck rolled down the lane and turned on the gravel road heading to Grayson. At the lane to my house, I stripped off the wet bandages and threw them into the ditch. The green goo had set in my wounds like a living poultice. When the truck stopped, the Wheat Pool elevator towered above me. A few seconds later, the smell of cigarette smoke drifted in the still air.

"Got two trucks ahead of you," Mr. Norman, the elevator man, called down.

"Don't hurry on my account," the driver called back.

I had one leg over the tailgate when I heard Dad's voice again. "... never come home last night. He's got his mother worried sick. She had me tramping all over hell looking for him. I told her he's probably just running with that Indian kid."

I dropped to the ground and glanced under the truck. Two pairs of legs stood ahead of the bumper.

"When I find that little —" Dad cussed, "I'll skin him alive."

"Okay!" Mr. Norman called. "You can dump 'er."

I stayed close behind the truck while Dad and the driver climbed into the cab and slammed their doors. The engine labored against its load, and as the truck let out a puff of smoke, I stepped past the tailgate and rounded the corner of the elevator.

In fifteen minutes, I was at Arthur's house.

There Are No Accidents

I went straight to the outhouse. It wasn't that I was trying to be unsociable, it was an emergency. I was just about finished when Arthur pulled the door open.

"I've been looking everywhere for you," he said.

"I guess you forgot to look here."

Arthur pinched his nose and closed the door. When I stepped out, he was sitting cross-legged on the path. I could tell by his face he'd had a hard night, too — one eye was puffy and nearly closed, and his lower lip was all swelled up.

"What happened?" I sat down beside him.

"You know that Mountie with the pimples?"

"Sure."

"He got to me just before Mr. Parks had me turned loose. I didn't tell the Mountie nothing but lies. He's probably still looking for you in Saskatchewan."

"Saskatchewan? I've never been there."

"I know," he said.

I told Arthur everything that had happened to me since he got thrown in jail. I showed him the dog bites and was just about to open my shirt when his grandpa came out of the house and stood in front of us.

"Take off your shirt," he said to me.

"Not again!" I said.

He pointed to my shirt.

I took it off.

He stared at the wound on my chest for a long while before he said, "Come with me."

I kept fearing I was headed back to that horrible barren hill in the middle of the prairie, but he didn't go nowhere but around the house, then sat in a long piece of shade. I sat near him. Arthur stood at the corner of the house. The old man never asked me what had happened during the night I spent on the hill. He just glanced at my chest.

"His name was Wolfleg," he said. "Wilfred Black was his Heavy Shield School name." The name the Anglicans gave him to start turning him into a white man.

While Arthur's grandpa spoke, I watched his eyes. There was something familiar, beyond him being Arthur's grandpa. Something that made me remember my night on the hill and the animal pacing the valley, keeping me from running away from whatever it was I was supposed to learn.

He told me Emma Howe and Wolfleg had had a child, that the Indians believed Old Man Howe sent Wolfleg to die in a war that was none of his concern, and then sent Wolfleg's son to another, and that Catface was Old Man Howe's great-grandson.

He pointed at the wound on my chest. "This doesn't make you an Indian."

"I know," I said, putting on my shirt. "It was just an accident."

Arthur's grandpa shook his head. "There are no accidents." He motioned to Arthur. "Go to Heavy Shield School," he said to both of us. "Get Catface and take him home."

He Runs Down the Hill Screaming

Arthur wouldn't look at me. He just kept his eyes on the dirt path we were following. We were nearly halfway to Heavy Shield School when I finally said, "I don't know why your grandpa told me."

"Yes you do. It's that thing on your chest."

"It's not a thing, Arthur."

"Well, it's not real."

I stopped, but Arthur went on a few more steps before he stopped and stared at the ground.

"What do you mean, not real?" I asked.

"If it doesn't come from a sun dance, it doesn't make you an Indian."

"I told your grandpa it was an accident. If I didn't get my stupid foot in Emma Howe's way, she would'a run right out the door with her stick poking at nothing but air. Arthur, I'm just Will. Except I got an Indian name now — He Runs Down the Hill Screaming."

A smile line formed on his cheek.

"It was really just a big sliver," I said, catching up to him. "It hardly even hurt."

Arthur pulled my shirt open. "Awfully deep for a sliver." When he poked it and I jumped, he added, "Pretty sore, too."

"Okay, but it still doesn't make me an Indian, unless you're looking for as worthless an Indian as there's ever been."

"It's not up to you to say what it means. Grandpa will decide that. And I'd say he's already spoken."

"I'm sorry, Arthur."

Arthur pulled my shirt closed with a rough jerk, but I could tell he was trying to hide how he felt, that he wished his grandpa had told *him* the story of Wilfred Black.

"Maybe with some help," Arthur said, "you could work your way up to being a fair Indian."

"I'd be proud to try."

Arthur buttoned my shirt and slapped me on the shoulder. "Let's go get Catface."

As we walked together toward Heavy Shield School, I thought about being an Indian. I decided that if I could be like any Indian who had ever lived, I'd be like Arthur.

We Need a Second Coming

We stopped in a caragana hedge along the topside of the driveway leading to the school grounds.

Ahead of us stood Heavy Shield School. There were no windows on our side, just a solid wall of red bricks about half the height of the Wheat Pool elevator and twice its width if you pushed the elevator over onto its side. The driveway went straight past the school. On the left was a large green lawn with a border of white flowers. On the right was the main entrance. Wide stairs went up to double doors on the second floor. At the base of the stairs was a neatly trimmed hedge covered in tiny yellow flowers.

Kratz, the third man who'd hunted Catface in the night, stepped out from the shadows and stood at the top of the stairs. He slid a pouch of tobacco from his shirt pocket, rolled a cigarette, and lit it. He blew out a half dozen puffs of smoke, then flicked the cigarette onto the driveway and disappeared inside.

"I'm getting a bad feeling," Arthur said. "Do you remember Grandpa saying Old Man Howe sent Wilfred Black and Samuel Black to die in wars?"

"Sure."

"Do you remember the bill in the post office?"

"The one we made?"

"No," Arthur said, "the Korea bill."

"What about it?"

"Howe is going to send Catface to Korea."

Before I could say anything back, Arthur swallowed hard, like he'd just figured out thirty-five years of meanness in a few seconds. "We've got to get him someplace safe," he added.

We stood with our backs against the cold bricks, took a big breath, then ran up the stairs. At the double doors, we stopped and listened.

Kids were singing a song about Emmanuel.

We slipped inside.

A long double-wide hall went from the entrance all the way to the chapel. A narrow hallway crossed in front of us. The halls were kind of dark. We held up for a moment and let our eyes get used to the low light. On the walls were pictures of religious people, government people and the old dead King. I didn't see any pictures of Chief Heavy Shield.

From the chapel, the song drifted out like an easy river.

The floor was covered with light-colored linoleum, as shiny as chrome on a new car. The air smelled like fresh paste wax. If there'd been any sunlight, it would've blinded the people inside.

Arthur pointed down the small hallway to the right.

Kratz was leaning against an open door. His back was to us, and he was talking to somebody inside the room.

Arthur rolled a rock in his hand. "Catface is close by," he whispered. "Or Kratz wouldn't be here."

I nodded.

Arthur stepped out into the middle of the hall and gave the rock a backhand toss. It made a smooth curve down the hall past Kratz's shoulder, bounced off the walls, hit the shiny floor, and rattled between the walls.

Kratz ducked, then tore after the rock.

"What the —" a voice shouted from inside the room.

We ran across the narrow hallway and on past the pictures of white people. A bright light poured from the chapel.

"Eeemmanuell," the kids sang together.

Twelve boys were singing. They had awfully beautiful voices.

"Slide," Arthur said with a quick, harsh whisper.

We dropped to the floor and slid on the waxed linoleum.

Our skin made little squeaking sounds as we slipped through the chapel doors and rolled in behind the last row of pews.

Arthur pulled up to the wall and took a big breath.

I lay on my back under a pew.

Arthur gave me the shush sign, then pointed.

Catface stood in the middle of the back row. He was about a foot taller than the rest. And he looked a little funny — all beat up and singing to Jesus about love. The Father was dressed in his long robe. The boys were wearing long robes, too. They looked like God's children.

"Why are they making Catface sing?" I asked. "He won't be doing any singing in Korea."

"The Father is driving out as much Indian as he can."

"So he'll be a better soldier."

Arthur gave me a look that meant an Indian was a better soldier all on his own. The white man's ways just made him weak.

I figured that's what Howe was hoping for.

"We can't just sit here and wait for them to finish," Arthur whispered.

"We need a distraction," I said, and crawled out from under the pew. "You got any rocks left?"

Arthur shook his head, but in a second he was crawling on his hands and knees to the small room in the near corner of the chapel. When he came back, he had a robe like the ones the Indian boys were wearing.

"Put this on," Arthur whispered.

I did as he said.

He pushed my sleeves up and stared at my arms. They were puffy and kind of blue with streaks of red at each tooth mark.

"That oughtta scare them," I said.

"We need more than scaring. We need a Second Coming."

"A what?"

"When were you last in church?" Arthur asked.

"Last Sunday."

"Maybe you should'a tried staying awake."

I went to give him a smart comeback, but then I understood his plan.

"Just hold your breath 'til I'm done," he said.

He half closed his eyes, made a painful-looking face, and started squeezing my hand. I was moaning and biting down on my teeth just as the boys got to a good and loud part of the song. Then I screamed, stood up, and staggered into the aisle, holding my arms over my head and singing like I had Jesus in my heart.

"Oh, I feel Him!" I cried. "He is with me. Oh, Emmanuel."

The Father stared at my raised hand and saw the blood coming from the hole. His eyes bugged out, and he crossed his heart.

The kids screamed all together, like it was part of their song.

A second later, they ran past me, still all together.

But the Father was getting wise. He pointed at me. "It's a sin to lie in the presence of the Almighty."

Arthur grabbed Catface and ran down the hall lined with important white people.

I followed, waving my arms over my head and hollering.

Kratz was looking out from the narrow hallway, trying to see what all the noise was. Behind him was another supervisor.

I made a jump for Kratz and moaned in a ghostly voice.

He fell as he tried to run toward me along the slippery hall.

"Come on!" Arthur hollered over his shoulder. "Findley and Howe will be after us soon."

"Coming!" I called, and ran down the big stairs.

Outside, Catface said, "I know a place," and pointed east.

Arthur took the lead, with Catface calling out directions. We ran straight across the lawn and through the border of white flowers. Bees and petals flew everywhere. When I jumped the flowers, the bees were good and mad, and they had me running hard when I reached the edge of the sand hill Heavy Shield School was built on.

The top edge had broken away and slid down the hill, making sharp jagged slices in the ground.

Arthur reached the edge, let out a "Yahoo!" and disappeared.

Catface hit the edge running hard, his robe flapping like he was Moses coming down from the mountain, and when he jumped, his long black hair streamed out behind him.

I got to the edge and slid, holding my sore arms above my head.

For the next fifteen minutes, we ran south, through open prairie with no cover. Anybody watching from Heavy Shield School would figure we were hitting for the river, where there was plenty of places to hide. But when we reached a shallow coulee, Catface called to follow the hills east. We were heading back toward Emma Howe's shack.

We ran and ran until I thought my lungs would catch fire and burn me up. I didn't know where we were — maybe five miles from the nearest road — when we turned up a ridge and headed out of the coulee.

In front of us was a lean-to shack.

Arthur kicked open the door and fell in.

Catface and I fell in behind him.

We lay there gasping for air. It seemed a day before I caught my breath, and about a week before I could talk.

Howe's Blood

Arthur glanced around the shack. "Whose place is this?"

"Mine," Catface said.

"Pretty nice," I said, acting like I wasn't tired.

Catface wiped his face with his sleeve, then got up and pulled the robe over his head. He was naked. I looked the other way as he took some old clothes from the floor and dressed.

The shack hadn't been used for a while. There was no firewood or flour or coffee or cans of food. But there were pictures — the same pictures I'd seen in Emma Howe's shack. I glanced at them, then back at Catface. He looked like Wilfred Black.

"Nice pictures," I said. "Where'd you get them?"

"They came in this." He dropped a stiff cloth rolled up like a tube and tied with a strip of leather.

"Did Arthur's grandpa take you to the hill? Did he make you stay all night with no clothes or fire or water or food? Was there a wolf in the valley? Did you think it'd kill you if you ran? Were you so scared you cried?"

Arthur and Catface were staring at me.

"What's the matter? What did I say?" I asked.

"Where's this hill?" Arthur asked.

"Somewhere close, I don't know. I just followed your grandpa."

"Well, you must'a walked a long way, because there's no hill like that around here," Arthur said.

"No wolves, either," Catface added.

I turned away from their stares. I didn't tell them that I was sure the hill had been in this exact spot. Arthur and Catface kept talking, but I didn't pay much attention to their words. I was trying to forget about how thirsty and hungry I felt. Before I could feel sorry about how much I hurt, Arthur raised his voice.

"What do you mean, ashamed? My grandpa has never been ashamed of anything in his life. He rode with Lame Bull and Crowfoot and Red Crow."

"He told me who these people are," Catface said and pointed to the pictures of Wilfred Black and Emma Howe and his own dad, Samuel Black. "He said the old Indians felt betrayed by my grandfather because he brought Howe's blood onto the reserve. I didn't say nothing about being ashamed. You said that yourself."

"It's the same thing."

"Maybe. Maybe not. I just told you what he said."

"What do you two think Howe's doing right now?" I asked in a rough voice. "I figure he's getting his men piled in the back of his truck, and he's coming after us. I don't figure he's arguing about some stupid word from thirty-five years ago."

They both looked at me.

"Now what?" I asked.

"There's something wrong with your eyes," Arthur said. "They're red like a campfire is burning inside."

"I hardly slept. I've been running for most of two days. I'm hungry and thirsty and I hurt all over. I'm worried Mom is going crazy because I didn't come home, I'm scared Dad will whup me good when I do get home, and now I got to listen to you two fight when we should be fighting Howe."

They blinked at me.

I wiped away my sweat and looked at the ceiling. It was made of straight young trees with a layer of sod on top. The trees that made up the ceiling were young when they were cut down. If they'd been left to stand, they'd be long dead from old age. Maybe it was the sweat in my eyes or something in the way they died, but they still seemed young.

Catface got up, pulled a new-looking paper bag from behind the door and set it between me and Arthur. He pulled out a loaf of bread and an old war canteen.

We split the bread equally, slice by slice, and drank the water in turn until it was gone. I slid the robe over my head and took the deed from under my belt. I handed it to Catface, still rolled in the stiff cloth and tied with the piece of leather.

"The wolf brought this to me the night I spent on the hill," I said. "As near as I could tell, he wasn't ashamed of anything."

Night Hunter

The sun was low in the sky when we left the lean-to and headed north to Emma Howe's shack. It seemed to me we were going the same way Leader had taken me.

We were maybe a quarter of the way when Catface said, "Howe could be there waiting for us."

"Nah, he'll be looking south, probably along the river," I said. "You made it pretty clear that's where we were headed when we ran out of the school."

"I hope Kratz tells Howe where we ran to."

"He will."

"But when that trail gets cold, Howe'll come looking for us at her shack."

Catface wouldn't call Emma Howe by her name, so I wasn't surprised that he couldn't call her "Grandma." I guess if I was raised by Fathers and Sisters and supervisors in a place like Heavy Shield School, I wouldn't know my own family either.

The sun was half a ball now, with the other half already set behind the mountains to the west. In another twenty minutes, Venus'd be shining bright.

I wondered what it was like to never know your dad or mom, to never go fishing in the spring when the pike were crazy to take a hook, to never have your mom bring you supper late in the night after you'd got the strap and figured nothing could ever make you feel better. I wondered what it was like to be hidden away because your family was ashamed of you. And I wondered what kind of dad could send the man his daughter loved off to war, hoping he'd get killed.

And then do it again — to his own blood, to his own grandson. Old Man Howe must have been awfully ashamed of his family.

I hadn't known Catface for more than a few hours, but I already had a good feeling about him. When we were about halfway and Venus was just coming to life, I made a decision. I decided I could stand to have Catface as my brother, and I figured my mom would welcome him, even if he was an Indian, and even if Dad wouldn't. So I said, "You can hide out at my place. If Emma doesn't want you."

Catface didn't say anything. He just stared straight ahead across the prairie and out into the coming night.

It looked like Arthur was going to say something, but nothing came but a little smile.

In the distance, the black dog was barking like he was chasing a jackrabbit. Thinking about him made my arms ache. I listened for Leader's bark. But all I could hear was a growling, tearing sound.

"Something's getting killed," Arthur said.

"Just a jackrabbit," I said quickly.

Catface was quiet except for a low moaning sound, maybe remembering Howe hunting him down.

"Maybe a deer?" I said.

"Whatever it is," Arthur said, "I hope it's big. So his belly's full before he catches our scent."

We were walking at a pretty easy pace considering we were on the run. Catface was in the middle. He was a little taller than Arthur, but then, he was older. I came to about his shoulder. He didn't look much like Arthur. Arthur was kind of thick with a wide face and short standing-up hair. Catface looked like he was made from long skinny bones. His neck was long, and his head was small, but it suited his body in general. His hair flowed over his shoulders and lay still on his back.

I wondered about his hair — why the white people at Heavy Shield School let him keep it long. Maybe it was his way of fighting back.

Catface changed as the darkness grew. His ears seemed to move, tracking the sounds. His breathing seemed to catch smells out of the air. He was becoming a night hunter.

A second dog had joined the black one, and together they were tearing at something, growling as they ate.

I listened carefully. I put them at the east side of the woods, maybe as far as the start of the wheat field. That wasn't good, because the breeze was moving from west to east. If we passed anywhere to the west of them, the wind would blow our scent right up their noses. They'd be on us in seconds.

Catface fixed on the sounds. "Let's get downwind," he said, and turned away from Grayson.

Farther east, we crossed the mound of rocks that held the railway tracks and headed over the strip of railway land, on to the fence bordering Catface's quarter section of wheat. There, we slipped under the barbed wire and walked into the grass along the field's edge.

Catface led the way, never once looking at his land.

The sound of the dogs grew louder. A fight broke out and snarled on for a few seconds.

Catface pointed to the base of the tracks. "Something's killed," he said, and kept on walking.

I couldn't get a good look. If the second dog was Sniffer, Howe was already at Emma's shack, waiting for us. He would likely have Albert Loewan and Fred and maybe even Kratz with him. I didn't want to think about Sergeant Findley being there, too. I felt outnumbered, just by the dogs.

I kept looking to the tracks, trying to see what Catface had pointed to. When I saw it, right across from us, I got an awful sick feeling in my stomach. Its tan-colored fur was still. A piece of flesh hung, folded back, dark against its body. Flies buzzed, then lifted, making a black cloud.

I couldn't see for sure because it was getting dark pretty fast. I was hoping it was a small deer, but I was afraid it was Leader. Maybe she got hit by a train. That would be quick at least.

Catface glanced at the shape half on the rocks and half in the prairie grass. "Too far away, and too dark to see," he said. "I hope the dogs are upwind of the shack. Then we can sneak right in."

They weren't. They were right in front of us, about a hundred yards east of the woods' edge. If I wanted to block somebody's way, that's where I would make my stand.

We've Got to Outsmart Him

The three of us lay shoulder to shoulder on the strip of grass between the wheat field and the barbed-wire fence. The breeze had turned into a light wind, rustling the wheat, blowing our scent back the way we'd come, so we could get closer to the dogs than I liked. But there wasn't enough wind to sneak past them. We'd need a tornado for that.

"They're down to the bones," Catface said.

"Almost finished," Arthur added.

"Probably a jackrabbit," Catface said.

"Not much of a supper for big dogs," Arthur said.

I glanced back. I couldn't see anything with my eyes, but my mind could see okay. The black dog had the animal down, and he was ripping big chunks from its body.

"If I had the pockfaced woman's ax," I said, "I'd show that black dog."

Arthur's shoulder moved against mine as he snickered. "If you had Old Man Howe's double-

160

barreled shotgun, you mean. And if you could shoot it without getting knocked on your rear end."

"I'd chop his head off."

"He'd eat you and the ax."

Catface gave us the shush sign. "He's too strong for us to fight, even if he was alone. But he's not. We've got to outsmart him."

Catface checked the wind. It was coming a little from the north now. With it came the smell of smoke from Emma Howe's cooking fire.

"Somebody could double back and get ahead of the dogs," I said. "Then run and draw them off. That would give the other two a chance to get into the woods."

Before Catface or Arthur could answer, I remembered the tunnel through the willows on the west edge of the woods. That gave me an idea.

Arthur was the fastest runner. He could outrun the dogs for a while, but eventually even he'd get caught. I wasn't much of a runner, but I knew where the tunnel was. If I got a good enough head start, I figured I could reach the tunnel before the dogs, crawl through it, then block it off and trap the dogs inside. By the time the dogs figured out that they could back up and go around the woods, I'd've reached Emma's shack.

I told Catface and Arthur about the secret tunnel and how Emma had got me clean away from the dogs earlier today.

"Sneaky lady," Catface said.

I went to get up, but Arthur put his hand on my back, then motioned to the woods. We listened. "Sounds pretty quiet. We'd hear Howe and his men if they were there. Move fast, and maybe we'll beat them."

I turned to Catface. "Emma doesn't know she's got a grandson. You'll have to show her you have the deed. But I figure she'll know you're kin as soon as she sees your face."

Actually, I figured Emma would drop dead when she saw Catface. He looked for all the world like Wilfred Black. I figured that was why Old Man Howe had him hidden away at Heavy Shield School for his whole life.

By the time they gave me the nod to go, I wished I'd never remembered the tunnel.

One of You Will Die

I crawled back along the fence line until I got about a hundred yards from where we'd seen the tan-colored body. There, I stood up and started running. In another quarter mile, I crossed the tracks, stopped and filled my pockets with egg-sized rocks, then hit for the reserve, thinking out my plan: After I got upwind, I'd have to make some noise to draw the dogs away from Arthur and Catface. I'd have to do it just right, so they would chase me but I would have enough time to get in and out of the tunnel ahead of them. The idea of getting chewed up worse than I already was had my heart pounding against my ribs so hard and loud that I almost walked right into a cactus patch.

I counted off four hundred paces, turned west, and walked parallel to the railway tracks. It seemed like I had just left Arthur and Catface when the tall shape of the trees grew on my right. The woods seemed a horrible black as I crouched back to the railway tracks.

Over Grayson, Venus had risen.

I took a deep breath, made a secret wish, and started chucking rocks.

The dogs made a few curious barks.

Then I threw a rock that hit the rail so hard it cracked like a rifle shot.

That brought a burst of quick angry barks.

They were after me.

I fell down the rise of rocks, stumbled across the railway land, and jumped for the fence. A barb caught my shirt behind my shoulder and tore it into two long strips.

The dark shapes loped down the tracks. They were already halfway to getting me and I'd just started.

I followed the woods' edge, looking right, searching the dark twisted willows for the tunnel.

The dogs leaped from the tracks and jumped the barbed wire, made loud grunts as they landed, and started through the grass.

I turned into the woods and ran twenty yards before I dropped to my knees at the base of the willows. I grabbed the branches and shook them. But there was no opening. I jerked my head left, then right. The thistle flowers I'd run through earlier today were gone.

I was on the wrong path.

I headed back out of the woods, ran north away from the dogs, and took the next path. It was wrong, too.

The dogs sniffed and grunted.

I doubled back, running right toward them, and on past both paths, half gasping, half choking. When I saw the light-blue flowers, the dogs were nearly on me. I turned into the woods. The smell of stinkweed filled the air. The flowers exploded around me.

The dogs shot from the blue cloud. Their teeth snapped like steel leg traps.

One of them bit my heel.

I jerked out of my shoe and ran on. The tunnel flashed into sight just as the black dog hit me. My body arched forward as I fell to the base of the tunnel. In a second, both dogs were on me.

I rolled, hollering and kicking, among their legs.

The black dog bit, missed, and came up with a mouthful of rotten leaves.

Sniffer ripped at my lost shoe, then shook it hard in his mouth, the laces slapping his jowls like lines of stiff drool.

I clawed in the deadfall, caught a short heavy branch, and swung it blindly in the air. I missed, but the force of the swing rolled me away from the black dog as he bit again. With his head still bent to the ground, I took a two-handed swing and clubbed him square on the ear.

He stood for a second with his head hanging, frozen at an odd angle. Then he fell over. His muscles twitched. Before he could think of getting up, I rolled onto my side and kicked him in the ribs. His wind rushed out of him.

He was out cold.

I wound up to kick again, but Sniffer bit that shoe. I swung my club and hit my own foot. "Son of a —" I hollered.

Sniffer jerked backward.

I pushed away, feeling for the tunnel with my back. In another second, the black dog had come to and was halfway to standing. Sniffer stood beside him with my shoe still in his mouth.

They had me cornered and outnumbered.

I swung the club past their noses. "I'll kill you!" I hollered. I figured I was dead.

Then I heard hard breathing and grunting from inside the tunnel. I was hoping it was Arthur and Catface coming from the shack.

Then a growl came from deep in the darkness.

It was another dog.

I pushed my back up against the tunnel, blocking the dog's path, and got my club ready. "One of you will die!" I yelled, turning the club so a short jagged branch was down like the blade of an ax.

That's when I heard a yip and felt something cold and wet poke me in the back. I dropped to one side as Leader burst from the tunnel, running right between the black dog and Sniffer.

They stopped in mid-attack, paraded around Leader and sniffed.

That didn't last long. Sniffer tore into the black dog. In a second, they were on each other, snarling and biting as they rolled in the weeds.

Leader gave me a lick and disappeared back into the tunnel.

I grabbed my shoes and followed. Out the other end, I found a thick poplar stump and stuffed it deep into the tunnel entrance.

Ahead of us, truck brakes squealed. Doors banged open and slammed closed. Men cussed.

Indian Land

Leader headed down the overgrown trail toward the sound. I followed, glancing ahead into the darkness and back to the tunnel. Behind the willows, I could still hear the black dog and Sniffer fighting.

A truck engine rumbled. Headlights burned into the darkness, making twisted shadows among the trees.

"There he is again," a man called. "I told you I saw something."

"What are you talking about?" another man said. "I can't see nothing but a dog."

"If that's a dog, it's a big one," the first said.

"I know who this one is," the other said. "Get my gun. I've got a lesson that needs teaching."

Trees trashed and branches broke.

"Get outta my way!" the other hollered. "Let go, you crazy old fool."

A shotgun roared.

Buckshot ripped through the woods.

I broke from the trees into a clearing in time to see Albert Loewan break a thick branch across a man's back. The man dropped to the ground as Howe fired over his shoulder. A big chunk of damp earth flew into the air. Before Loewan could swing again, the man rolled over, got to one knee, and thrust a jagged piece of branch into Loewan's thigh.

Loewan staggered backward and fell behind the truck.

The man was standing now, his long gray hair half covering his face, his huge body towering over Howe.

It was Arthur's grandpa.

Howe slid two shells into the barrels and snapped the gun closed.

I stood on the edge of the clearing, my heart pounding, my legs shaking. I didn't know if I wanted to stay or run. But when Howe pushed the shotgun up against Arthur's grandpa's chest, I ran toward them, my eyes fixed on the gun.

"I thought I told you to get outta my way," Howe said.

I tripped and fell into the stiff underbrush. The branches jabbed into the wound on my chest. Tears ran down my cheeks. As I crawled, I pressed my hand over the wound, but it didn't help — the pain wasn't coming from there. It was coming from a place too deep to touch. For a reason I couldn't understand, the words of Big Lodge Pole filled my mind again. "Make my enemies brave and strong, so that if defeated, I will not be ashamed." I saw Arthur's grandpa now as a young man riding with Lame Bull.

Lame Bull leaned across his horse and pointed to a white soldier. *"Kaxtomo,"* he said. "The enemy."

"Kaxtomo!" I screamed at Howe.

In a single quick move, Arthur's grandpa jerked the shotgun from Howe's hands, broke the action, and dropped the emptied gun at Howe's feet.

When Howe bent to pick it up, Arthur's grandpa stepped on the barrel.

"Get off my land, you trespassing redskin!" Howe hollered up into his face.

"You're the trespasser," Arthur's grandpa said. "The deed you signed with Wilfred Black makes this Indian land."

I kept on running. *"Kaxtomo!"* I called again.

Howe's face was puffy and red with anger as he swung at me. I turned my head, and he missed and stumbled into Arthur's grandpa. He steadied himself and swung again. I didn't even have to move. He missed again, and landed on his back.

"I've got ways to get to a man that you've never dreamed of," Howe cussed and pulled himself up.

As he took one last swing, Arthur's grandpa grabbed Howe's fist, lifted him up, and backed him into the truck. "Go home before the boy hurts you," he said, and pushed him behind the wheel.

Old Man Howe let out a stream of cusses that made Loewan stop groaning and stand in the truck box to look over the cab. When Howe jammed the truck into gear and drove off, Loewan fell onto the roof.

Behind us, Arthur and Catface were hollering as they came running through the trees.

Arthur's grandpa stepped into the woods just as Arthur and Catface broke into the clearing.

"Is Old Man Howe here?" Arthur asked.

"No," I said. "But he was."

"Has he gone to get more men?" Catface asked. "Is Findley coming?"

"We better get to Miss Emma's shack before it's too late," Arthur said.

As Arthur and Catface turned back, I stood in the darkness, watching where the old Indian had passed become fainter and fainter, until his large shape slowly stooped to the earth, and he disappeared into night.

You Can Go Home Now

When I got to the shack, Arthur and Catface were sitting on the ground outside the door. Inside, Emma Howe was softly crying.

"She's crazy," Catface said.

"She's scared, is all," I told him, sitting down beside him.

Arthur mouthed "Crazy."

"Where's Pockface?" I asked him.

"Holding the door closed."

"Wanna try the window?"

"She's got the ax."

"I suppose she does," I said. "And there's those heavy shutters."

"She doesn't want me around," Catface finally said.

"Emma?" I asked. "It's Old Man Howe who doesn't want you around. Emma doesn't even know you. Her dad saw to that."

"Shut up out there!" Pockface hollered. Then she punched the door. "I'll come out there and put my blade through your scrawny necks."

"She's sitting on the floor to keep the door closed?" I asked.

"Yeah," Arthur said.

"We'll need a tractor to move her."

Leader walked out of the dark, her head bent toward the ground. But I could tell by the way she wagged her tail and looked awfully satisfied that the bashfulness was just an act. I guess she'd been keeping the dogs fighting. Maybe they'd killed each other.

She came over and leaned on my leg. It took all of two seconds until she was asleep. I stroked her side, the same tan color as the dead animal lying by the railway tracks. A lump came up in my throat.

I patted her shoulder and on down her chest. Her heart beat nice and easy. She made a sleepy sigh.

The longer I sat, the more I didn't want to move. All around us, the woods were quiet, like fighting men didn't matter at all to the night. Overhead, a meteor burned a long curve through the darkness. I was thinking about Mom, how she'd be worried sick that I was dead in a ditch. Maybe she was wishing on that meteor that I was home.

Before long, Old Man Howe would be back with Sergeant Findley. I'd get a good bawling out and the strap, Arthur'd get thrown back in jail, and Catface'd get shipped off to Korea so he could get killed and be with his dad and grandpa.

My body had stiffened from all the running and fighting. I felt like I might never move again. But when a set of headlights flashed through the woods, I tried to get up.

Catface held his hands out at his sides. "I'm finished running."

Arthur just looked at his feet.

We sat there waiting for Sergeant Findley to haul us away.

The headlights searched back and forth through the woods as the car made the last few turns in the trail. A black shape pulled up and stopped. The motor purred. Then the lights went out and the engine died.

The door opened, and the inside light lit the driver's face. It was Jane Howe. Her eyes were all red and puffy. She looked like she'd been crying since I'd seen her shamed by her father as she sat in his truck.

We stood as she walked between us and stopped at the door. "Will," she whispered, "I can't remember her name."

"Alice," I whispered back.

"Alice, it's Jane. Emma's sister. You can go home now."

Leader was awake, standing by my leg. I had my hand on her head and was petting her without thinking about it.

As Jane Howe spoke, her hand went searching around in the darkness — kind of low, like she didn't want us to see — until she found Catface. Her hand moved down his arm.

"I'll take care of things from now on." Jane had found Catface's hand and was holding it.

The pockfaced woman opened the door and stood in the lamplight, the blade of her ax tapping against her boot top.

"You can go now," Jane said. "I'll take care of my sister."

"You don't tell me nothing."

"I do now," Jane said, and held up the deed that Catface had been holding.

Pockface stared straight ahead as she walked past us toward the reserve.

In that moment, the day came together. Catface and Emma and Jane would be a family. And if Old Man Howe didn't like it, he'd have to be ashamed all alone.

I Made a Wish for You Tonight

Mom cleaned up my arms and hands. When she wanted to get Dr. Wilcox to stitch up my chest, I said I'd run away if he tried. Mom let my words go, mixed up a fresh poultice even stinkier than Emma's, and wrapped my other wounds in new bandages. When she finished and was sure I wasn't going to die, she gave me a good bawling out.

"Dad's been looking all over for you. A driver for Howe said he'd seen you over by the irrigation pond. Dad figured you drowned."

"I can swim, Mom."

"Don't sass me," she said, pointing her finger. "Dad'll give you a good strapping when he gets back."

"I'm sorry for not coming home."

"We were scared you'd got hurt." Mom's voice got kind of shaky. "That you were lying in a ditch somewhere."

She turned her back and touched the water-bucket handle.

"You want me to fetch some water?"

"You boys don't know what it's like to be a mom." Her lips twitched. "I'd die if one of my boys got killed."

I reached for her hand, and our fingers wrapped so tight it felt like they were one thing. My brother, Tim, would tease me and so would Dad, but I didn't care. It felt pretty good.

"I made a wish for you tonight," I said. "On a shooting star."

"You wished I'd make bread pudding?"

"No, it wasn't a food wish."

"Well, maybe that I'd wash your clothes more?"

"Mom."

"Hoe your potatoes?"

"It was just for you."

She gave me a look that said "Don't tease a mom who's spent most of two days and nights sick with worry."

I knew you shouldn't tell a wish or you risk not getting it, but I told it anyway. "I want you to get your little fence. The white one you talk to Dad about. And electricity for the house and an inside toilet and a new dress once a year."

"That must'a been a pretty big shooting star."

"Biggest I ever saw."

We stood there for a while longer. She had a faint smile, and she was taking long slow breaths. In the window, her reflection looked soft and young.

A light crossed the glass, and she turned and looked down the lane. "Here comes Dad and Tim. You go to bed. I'll talk to them."

"But I'm hungry. What about supper?"

"I'll bring some to you a little later."

I headed for bed. Behind me, I could hear Tim and Dad tramping into the kitchen.

"I can't find him no place," Dad said.

"He's in bed."

"He better be half dead or I'll make him wish he was."

"He got attacked by a dog. He's hurt."

"Bad?" Dad asked.

"Too bad for strapping."

"A dog? How come he didn't come home?"

"He got treed. He had to stay in the tree 'til the dog left."

"What kind of dog sits under a tree for two days?"

"I don't understand dogs."

"Was it crazy with rabies or something?"

"No, nothing like that."

I could hear Dad walking back and forth in the kitchen. I'd bet he was scratching his head.

"At least he's not drowned in the irrigation pond," Tim said. "Now you won't have to drag it like Grandpa did to find Aunt Molly."

There was a loud slap.

"Shut your mouth!" Dad shouted.

"I only meant —"

"Are you deaf, boy?"

"Jim," Mom said. "Tim meant no harm."

"I know. It's that other one who's causing this family misery."

"You were just scared, is all."

"I'm not scared of nothing," Dad said. "For all I care, let him drown. He can drown all he wants. Go be with Molly. Damn his hide. Goddamn his hide."

The kitchen became awfully quiet. A few minutes later, Tim came into the bedroom, undressed and crawled into his bed. Cigarette smoke drifted in from the kitchen.

"Want some tea?" Mom asked after a while.

"Okay," Dad said.

I lay awake for a long time. Tim was asleep, breathing long slow breaths. The kitchen was still when I got up and stood by the crack in the door. Mom was sitting on the floor beside Dad's chair, her arms crossed on his lap, her head resting quietly in the cradle of her hands. Dad ran his hand through Mom's hair as he gazed across the living room at the narrow opening in the doorway, where I hid in the darkness.

It Made Me Feel Kind of Small

It was noon when I finally got up.

Mom unrolled my bandages and looked at my bites. "Dad should be able to strap you in a few days." She grinned, wrapped me up again, and sent me outside. "Don't go getting killed by no dogs!" she hollered out the door.

"Aw, Mom, I can climb a tree pretty good."

I could hear her laughing.

I walked to me and Arthur's star-watching spot behind the outhouse, lay in the soft cover of grass, and rested my head on the stuffed burlap sack we used for a pillow. The sun burned down on me. The new moon had moved to the east to become the thin line of light at dusk — a two-day moon — on its way to full. I wondered how many millions of times the moon had done just that.

Thinking that made me feel kind of small.

I was half asleep when Mom came out and got the clothes from the line. She sang a quiet, mournful song as she worked. I didn't know it by name so much as how it made me feel.

Lately, when I felt bad about one thing, I started remembering everything that ever made me feel bad. In a second, I was thinking about Aunt Molly. She was floating facedown in the irrigation pond, her white nightgown spread out around her, Dad hollering from the shore, "Damn your hide! Goddamn your hide!"

At about four o'clock, Mom came out and called, "Are you going to do anything but sleep?"

"Yeah. I'm going to go look at stars with Arthur."

"Not for the whole night, I hope."

"Nah, just for a while."

"Don't go near any rabid dogs."

"Okay, Mom."

Mom closed the door, and in a few minutes, she came out carrying a flour sack. "Here, I made you some supper. And some for Arthur too."

I untied the knot. Inside were two sandwiches made from thick slices of freshly baked bread with butter and a big piece of hamburger. Under the sandwiches was a thermos of coffee. And under everything else was a piece of rolled-up rag about the size of a bar of soap. It looked nice and neat, like it was a gift.

"Don't forget to share with Arthur."

"I won't," I said as I dusted off my pants. "Do you suppose Dad would mind if I borrowed the shovel and some tools?"

"He thinks you lose more than you bring back."

"I'll be careful."

"Okay."

I started for the toolshed.

"Dad said to check that pile of CPR fence posts by the graveyard, make sure they're stacked good," Mom said. "He wants to throw them on the pickup and bring them home. And don't forget to gather up all the staples — Dad'll be hot if he gets a flat tire. If you do an extra-good job, maybe he'll go easy on your strapping."

"Okay. I'll check. I was planning to go by there anyway."

"Be careful."

I waved to Mom. "If I see a crazy dog," I said, "I'll jump in the irrigation pond."

"I don't know why I bother."

I headed up the lane with the flour sack tied to the shovel handle, resting on my shoulder, and my poor shoes flopping around on my feet. As I walked, I sang a made-up song about Emmanuel.

I Am Not Ashamed

When I got to the end of our lane, where the main gravel road crossed in front of me, I saw the three-ton grain truck coming from town.

When it got close enough, I could see two men standing in the back with the wind blowing their long hair. Neither of them was Arthur's dad.

I started across the road. The horn honked. Thinking Albert Loewan was going to run me down, I jumped for the ditch. The horn let out a bunch of honks, like it was talking.

Behind the wheel was Arthur's dad. He stuck his arm out the open window and gave the roof a booming slap, then waved and turned up the lane. I guess that table and chairs still needed paying for. I ran so he could see me in his side mirror and gave him a big wave.

He shifted gears, built up speed, and headed to Howe's farm.

I turned up the gravel road and walked to town. At the Mountie barracks, I stood and looked at

Lowhorn's cell. I'd told Mom all about how Lowhorn had saved Arthur and me from getting caught by Sergeant Findley. She said I was a lucky boy to know such good people.

I took out the little package that looked like a bar of soap. I turned it over in my hand, then put it to my nose and sniffed it. My thoughts were right. It was tobacco. Probably papers too. I tossed it. It sailed through the air and slipped free and easy between the bars.

Maybe Lowhorn was there, or maybe he was in Spy Hill. I didn't wait around.

I was at the end of the alley when I smelled the cigarette smoke and heard a hand slap the outside bricks. Maybe Lowhorn was saying it was good to have a friend like me.

When I got to the library, Jane Howe was just backing her car out into the street. Beside her was Emma, and in the backseat was Catface. Stacked all around him were bags of groceries and dry goods.

I went to wave, but stopped. They wouldn't even notice me. They were looking no place but at one another, talking and laughing like they'd been a family forever.

I walked to the library door and stood looking through the glass. In my mind, I could see Jane's reflection standing behind me and I heard her say again, "Everyone has some shameful thing in their lives."

I switched the shovel and my sack of food to the other shoulder, turned down Main Street and headed west along the railway tracks to the pile of fence posts I'd stacked. Dad had got them from the CPR just for hauling them away.

I pulled the roll of rusty barbed wire from the pile and dropped it over the shovel handle, gathered up some loose staples, and put them in my pocket. Then I dug through the posts until I found the best two.

Dry cedar is a pretty light wood. That's good because I only planned to make one trip.

The sun was hot, and I was sweating when I rested the posts on either side of the narrow depression where the earth had settled over Aunt Molly's grave. I sat with my elbows on my knees and my chin cupped in my hands. I couldn't read the faded writing on the wooden cross, but I knew I was in the right spot. It was the only one outside the graveyard.

I dug two holes at the foot of her grave, set the posts, and tamped them with the shovel handle. I strung four rows of wire between them and stapled the ends to the two posts bordering the graveyard. Then I pushed down the wire in the main graveyard's fence and stepped through. I looked at Aunt Molly's wooden cross leaning in the pale clay soil, all alone inside its new fence.

I pulled Dad's old wire cutters from my pocket, and one by one I snipped the four rows of wire barring her from the graveyard.

As the last wire fell, I could see Dad sitting at our kitchen table, Mom at his side with her arms crossed on his lap, her head resting in the cradle of her hands and him stroking her hair.

And I said, "I am not ashamed."

About the Author

"I pretty much daydream whenever I feel like it."
— Ted Stenhouse

Born into poverty in a small Manitoba town in the 1950s, Ted Stenhouse discovered the power of his imagination at a young age. In those days, he daydreamed a lot — especially during class.

School was very difficult for Stenhouse, and reading proved to be one of his greatest challenges. "I remember one day we all had to take turns reading aloud," says Stenhouse. "Even with my head down, I could see each kid stand up and read. My face felt like it was on fire. Then it was a Native boy's turn. He was almost as poor a reader as me. We became good friends after that day."

High school was a nightmare. "By the end of grade eleven I was so far behind," he states, "I couldn't see the end of it. In grade twelve I gave up and became a full-time daydreamer. In the spring of that year, I was kicked out for good."

After stints as a maintenance man, engineering department superintendant and a building superintendent, Stenhouse felt it was time to broaden his education; he enrolled first in community college and then at the University of Alberta.

There, Stenhouse met Teya Rosenberg, his first-year English professor. She was studying for her Ph.D. in children's literature and she encouraged Stenhouse with her devotion to her work. "I didn't know it on my first day of classes," remarks Stenhouse, "but her enthusiasm for all literature was going to change my life. From then on I would be a daydreamer with a purpose."

Literature, reading and writing — the things that he dreaded most in school — would now give him the most joy. He began studying creative writing through the University of Iowa. His days were filled with reading about the craft, studying other authors' styles, and, of course, writing.

A Dirty Deed is Stenhouse's second novel. He is currently hard at work on his next project — after having enjoyed a bit of daydreaming.

Also by Ted Stenhouse

Across the Steel River

When we first saw it, I thought it was a dog, but Arthur said it was a man. He said it like he thought I didn't know anything about anything. If I hadn't been so scared I would have been mad.

Arthur is right — it *is* a man, badly beaten and left for dead. But it's not just any man. A decorated soldier back from the Second World War, Yellowfly lives on the reserve across the tracks from Grayson.

The local police decide a train is the cause of Yellowfly's injuries and most of the townsfolk tend to agree. But Will and Arthur know better — and realize they'll have to pursue the case on their own.

The two boys have been friends forever, but folks figure it won't last. After all, it's 1952 in a small prairie town — whites and Indians always outgrow their friendships.

As they search for justice, Will and Arthur discover that true brotherhood sometimes calls for sacrifice. And that courage, like cowardice, can take many forms.

"A thoughtful, discerning picture of the difficulties of standing up for what is right." — *Booklist*

"A sensitive portrayal." — *School Library Journal*